The Time of the Doves

A NOVEL BY

MERCE RODOREDA

TRANSLATED BY

DAVID H. ROSENTHAL

GRAYWOLF PRESS

First paperback edition, 1986
Reprinted by arrangement with
Taplinger Publishing Co., Inc.
132 West 22nd Street, New York, NY 10001

ISBN 978-0-915308-75-0
Library of Congress Catalog Card Number 85-80976

Publication of this volume is made possible in part
by a grant from the National Endowment for the Arts.

Published by Graywolf Press
2402 University Avenue
Suite 203
Saint Paul, Minnesota 55114

15 14 13 12 11 10 9 8

To J. P.

Translator's Note

Mercè Rodoreda is the most widely-read and, many think, the best contemporary Catalan prose writer. Born in 1909 in Barcelona, she was a passionate reader even as a little girl and came of age as a writer shortly after the proclamation of the Spanish Republic. Between 1932 and 1937 she published prolifically—five novels, plus numerous shorter pieces in periodicals like *Mirador, La Rambla,* and *Publicitat*—and was considered one of the most promising young Catalan authors.

With the end of the Civil War in 1939, however, this whole universe collapsed. Catalan books were burned, Catalan newspapers suppressed, and offices were hung with signs saying NO LADRES, HABLA EL IDIOMA DEL IMPERIO ESPAÑOL (don't bark, speak the language of the Spanish empire). Rodoreda found herself, along with many other refugees, in France—first living in Paris, and then fleeing south before Hitler's invading armies. In an interview published in the magazine *Serra d'Or,* she describes her state of mind during this period:

> The prewar world seemed unreal to me, and I still haven't reconstructed it. And the time I spent! Everything burned inside, but imperceptibly it was becoming a little anachronistic. And perhaps this is what hurt most. I couldn't have written a novel if they'd beaten it out of me. I was too disconnected

from everything, or maybe too terribly bound up with everything, though that might sound like a paradox. In general, literature made me feel like vomiting. I could only stand the greats: Cervantes, Shakespeare, Dostoyevsky. I'm sure I've never been as lucid as I was then, possibly because I hardly ate anything.

Nonetheless, Rodoreda eventually did begin writing again and, in 1957, produced her first book in twenty years, *Vint-i-dos contes (Twenty-two Stories)*. Five years later *The Time of the Doves (La Plaça del Diamant* in its original Catalan edition) appeared. Since then she has published regularly, while *The Time of the Doves* is now in its seventeenth edition. Twelve of these editions came out during Franco's dictatorship, despite official efforts to stamp out the Catalan language and culture. The book has been translated into ten languages and will shortly be filmed by Spanish television. Its success is a testimony both to its artistic merit and its extraordinary power to evoke the psychic and material ravages of our century.

In a sense, *The Time of the Doves* is the story of most Spaniards during the 1930s and 1940s. But more profoundly, it explores what it feels like to be an ordinary woman in a Mediterranean country. Rodoreda uses a stream-of-consciousness technique to place us directly inside Natalia's sensibility, yet her technique is so subtle that we are aware only of the flow of Natalia's feelings. The author's literary skill never draws attention to itself. Instead, the heroine's mind plays obsessively over certain images, returning to them again and again until they become protagonists in her agony. Painfully sensitive but unable to objectify what she feels, Natalia is choked rather than educated by her experiences. A victim of history, she nonetheless lacks any historical sense. The book's densely-packed detail gives *The Time of the Doves* an almost hypnotic intensity and draws the reader into Natalia's private horrors.

> And without thinking I started walking again and the walls carried me along more than my own footsteps and I turned into the Plaça del Diamant: an empty box made of old buildings with the sky for a top. And I saw some little shadows fly across the top and all the buildings started rippling like they were in a pool and someone was slowly stirring it and the walls on the buildings stretched upwards and leaned toward each other and the hole at the top got smaller and started turning into a funnel and I felt something in my hand and it was Mateu's hand and a satin-tie dove landed on his shoulder and I've never seen one before but its feathers shimmered like a rainbow and I heard a storm coming up like a whirlwind inside the funnel which was almost closed now and I covered my face with my arms to protect myself from I don't know what and I let out a hellish scream. A scream I must have been carrying around inside me for many years, so thick it was hard for it to get through my throat and with that scream a little bit of nothing trickled out of my mouth, like a cockroach made of spit . . . and that bit of nothing that had lived so long trapped inside me was my youth and it flew off with a scream of I don't know what . . . letting go?

To place *The Time of the Doves* and its author in their proper perspective, the American reader may find some historical background useful. Catalan is a language spoken by approximately seven million people, some of whom live in the Balearic Islands, others in a small strip of

Southern France that includes Perpinyà (Perpignan), and others in Spain proper, from Alacant (Alicante) to the French border and between the Mediterranean Sea and Aragon. A Romance language, Catalan is closer to Provençal and Italian than to Castilian (the language normally called "Spanish").

The most interesting Catalan literature is of two periods: the late Middle Ages and early Renaissance, and from around 1870 to the present. The first era produced such outstanding writers as the lyric poet Ausiàs March (ca. 1397-1459) and the novelist Joanot Martorell (ca. 1410-1468), whose masterpiece *Tirant lo Blanc* was described by Cervantes as "the best book in the world." During the past century, Catalonia has produced an astonishing body of artistic work. In the visual arts, the genius of figures like Pablo Picasso, Joan Miró, Salvador Dalí, Antoni Tàpies and Antoni Gaudí is universally recognized. Catalan writing is of equally high quality, but the world has been slower to become aware of its virtues—partly due to a lack of good translations, and partly because of the Franco government's deliberate suppression.

Catalans were on the losing side in the Spanish Civil War, and immediately afterwards were forbidden to speak their language outside the home. For writers like Rodoreda, who did not reestablish her residence in Spain until 1979, the fate of Catalan was a matter of artistic survival. A writer's native language is normally his or her only medium of expression. If a language dies or is killed, then the writer also dies. Thus, as with many Catalan authors, her personal story is of a kind of death followed by a recent and partial rebirth.

Since the end of the Franco era, Catalans have moved

steadily towards self-rule. They now have a bilingual government and a newly approved Statute of Autonomy. The first elections to the Catalan parliament recently took place. The study of Catalan is now obligatory in the schools, and Catalan daily newspapers and radio stations are free to operate for the first time since 1939. Thanks to novelists like Rodoreda and poets like J. V. Foix, Salvador Espriu, and Vicent Andrés Estellés, Catalan literature has remained as vital as ever. One hopes that these writers will now begin to receive more recognition in the United States. Perhaps the following quotation from the French critic Michel Cournot in *Le Nouvel Observateur* will suggest the prestige Rodoreda has already achieved in Europe:

> One feels that this little working woman in Barcelona has spoken on behalf of all the hope, all the freedom, and all the courage in the world. And that she has just uttered forth one of the books of most universal relevance that love—let us finally say the word—could have written.

David H. Rosenthal
Barcelona, 1980

My dear, these things are life.

—GEORGE MEREDITH

Julieta came by the pastry shop just to tell me that, before they raffled off the basket of fruit and candy, they'd raffle some coffeepots. She'd already seen them: lovely white ones with oranges painted on them. The oranges were cut in half so you could see the seeds. I didn't feel like dancing or even going out because I'd spent the day selling pastries and my fingertips hurt from tying so many gold ribbons and making so many bows and handles. And because I knew Julieta. She felt fine after three hours' sleep and didn't care if she slept at all. But she made me come even though I didn't want to, because that's how I was. It was hard for me to say no if someone asked me to do something. I was dressed all in white, my dress and petticoats starched, my shoes like two drops of milk, my earrings white enamel, three hoop bracelets that matched the earrings, and a white purse Julieta said was made of vinyl with a snap shaped like a gold shellfish.

When we got to the square, the musicians were already playing. The roof was covered with colored flowers and paper chains: a chain of paper, a chain of flowers. There were flowers with lights inside them and the whole roof was like an umbrella turned inside out, because the ends of the chains were tied much higher up than the middle where they all came together. My petticoat had a rubber waistband I'd had a lot of trouble putting on with a crochet hook that could barely squeeze through. It was fastened with a little button and a loop of string and it dug into my skin. I probably already had a red mark around my waist, but as soon as I started breathing harder I began to feel like I was being martyred. There were asparagus plants around the bandstand to keep the crowd away, and the plants were decorated with flowers tied together with tiny wires. And the musicians with their jackets off, sweating. My mother had been dead for years and couldn't give me advice and my father had remarried. My father remarried and me without my mother whose only joy in life had been to fuss over me. And my father remarried and me a young woman all alone in the Plaça del Diamant waiting for the coffeepot raffle and Julieta shouting to be heard above the music "Stop! You'll get your clothes all wrinkled!" and before my eyes the flower-covered lights and the chains pasted on them and everybody happy and while I was gazing a voice said right by my ear, "Would you like to dance?"

Without hardly realizing, I answered that I didn't know how, and then I turned around to look. I bumped into a face so close to mine that I could hardly see what it looked like, but it was a young man's face. "Don't worry," he said. "I'm good at it. I'll show you how." I thought about poor Pere, who at that moment was shut up in the basement of the Hotel Colón cooking in a white apron, and I was dumb enough to say:

"What if my fiancé finds out?"

He brought his face even closer and said, laughing, "So young and you're already engaged?" And when he laughed his lips stretched and I saw all his teeth. He had little eyes like a monkey and was wearing a white shirt with thin blue stripes, soaked with sweat around the armpits and open at the neck. And suddenly he turned his back to me and stood on tiptoe and leaned one way and then the other and turned back to me and said, "Excuse me," and started shouting, "Hey! Has anyone seen my jacket? It was next to the bandstand! On a chair! Hey . . ." And he told me they'd taken his jacket and he'd be right back and would I be good enough to wait for him. He began shouting, "Cintet . . . Cintet!"

Julieta, who was wearing a canary-yellow dress with green embroidery on it, came up from I don't know where and said, "Cover me. I've got to take off my shoes. . . . I can't stand it anymore." I told her I couldn't move because a boy who was looking for his jacket and was determined to dance with me had told me to wait for him. And Julieta said, "Then dance, dance. . . ." And it was hot. Kids were setting off firecrackers and rockets in the street. There were watermelon seeds on the ground and near the buildings watermelon rinds and empty beer bottles and they were setting off rockets on the rooftops too and from balconies. I saw faces shining with sweat and young men wiping their faces with handkerchiefs. The musicians happily playing away. Everything like a decoration. And the two-step. I found myself dancing back and forth and, like it was coming from far away though really it was up close, I heard his voice: "Well, so she *does* know how to dance!" And I smelled the strong sweat and faded cologne. And those gleaming monkey's eyes right next to mine and those ears like little medallions. That rubber waistband digging into my waist and my dead mother couldn't advise me, because I told him my fiancé was a cook at the Colón and he laughed and said he felt sorry for him because by New Year's I'd be his wife and his queen and we'd be dancing in the Plaça del Diamant.

"My queen," he said.

And he said by the end of the year I'd be his wife and I hadn't even looked at him yet and I looked him over and then he said, "Don't look at me like that or they'll have to pick me up off the ground," and when I told him he had eyes like a monkey he started laughing. The waistband was like a knife in my skin and the musicians "TararI tararI!" And I couldn't see Julieta anywhere. She'd disappeared. And me with those eyes in front of me that wouldn't go away, as if the whole world had become those eyes and there was no way to escape them. And the night moving forward with its chariot of stars and the festival going on and the fruitbasket and the girl with the fruitbasket, all in blue, whirling around. . . . My mother in Saint Gervasi Cemetery and me in the Plaça del Diamant. . . . "You sell sweet things? Honey and jam . . ." And the musicians, tired, putting things in their cases and taking them out again because someone had tipped them to play a waltz and everyone spinning around like tops. When the waltz ended people started to leave. I said I'd lost Julieta and he said he'd lost Cintet and that when we were alone and everyone shut up in their houses and the streets empty we'd dance a waltz on tiptoe in the Plaça del Diamant . . . round and round. . . He called me Colometa, his little dove. I looked at him very annoyed and said my name was Natalia and when I said my name was Natalia he kept laughing and said I could have only one name: Colometa. That was when I started running with him behind me: "Don't get scared . . . listen, you can't walk through the streets all alone, you'll get robbed. . . ." and he grabbed my arm and stopped me. "Don't you see you'll get robbed, Colometa?" And my mother dead and me caught in my tracks and that waistband pinching, pinching, like I was tied with a wire to a bunch of asparagus.

And I started running again. With him behind me. The stores shut with their blinds down and the windows full of silent things like inkwells and blotters and postcards and dolls and clothing on display and aluminum pots and needlepoint patterns. . . . And we came out on the Carrer Gran and me running up the street and him behind me and both of us running and years later he'd still talk about it sometimes: "The day I met Colometa in the Plaça del Diamant she suddenly started running and right in front of the streetcar stop, blam! her petticoat fell down."

The loop broke and my petticoat ended up on the ground. I jumped over it, almost tripping, and then I started running again like all the devils in hell were after me. I got home and threw myself on the bed in the dark, my girl's brass bed, like I was throwing a stone onto it. I felt embarrassed. When I got tired of feeling embarrassed, I kicked off my shoes and untied my hair. And Quimet, years later, still talked about it as if it had just happened: "Her waistband broke and she ran like the wind. . . ."

It was very mysterious. I'd put on my pink dress, a little too light for the weather, and I got goosebumps waiting for Quimet on a corner. After I'd been standing around for a while doing nothing, I felt like someone was watching me from behind some shutters, because I saw the slats on one side move a little. Quimet and I had agreed to meet near Güell Park. A man came out of the building with a revolver in his belt and holding a shotgun and went by, brushing against my skirt and calling out, "Meki, meki. . . ."

Someone pushed down the slats, the shutters flew open and a man in pajamas went "Pst! pst!" and, crooking his finger, motioned me to come closer. To make sure, I pointed to myself and, looking at him, whispered, "Me?" Without hearing he understood and nodded his head, which was very handsome, and I crossed the street and came closer. When I was right below the balcony he said, "Come on in and we'll take a little nap."

I blushed bright red and went away furious—mainly with myself—and feeling very nervous because I could feel him staring right into my back through my clothes and skin. I stood where the young man in pajamas couldn't see me but I was afraid that, since I was half hidden, it was Quimet who wouldn't see me. I decided to wait and see what happened because it was the first time we'd arranged to meet outside a park. That morning at work I'd been thinking so much about the afternoon that I'd done all kinds of dumb things. I felt so nervous I thought I'd go out of my mind. Quimet had said we'd meet at three-thirty and he didn't show up till four-thirty; but I didn't say anything because I thought maybe I hadn't heard him right and it was me who'd made a mistake and since he didn't say even half a word of apology . . . I was afraid to tell him my feet hurt from standing up so long because I was wearing very hot patent leather shoes and how a young man had taken liberties with me. We started walking up the hill without saying a single wretched word and when we got to the top I didn't feel cold anymore and my skin went back to being smooth like usual. I wanted to tell him I'd broken up with Pere, that everything was settled now. We sat down on a stone bench in a corner out of sight, between two slender trees with long, thin leaves, and a blackbird who kept flying up into them and went from one to the other giving harsh little chirps. We'd sit for a while without seeing him and then he'd fly down onto the ground just when we'd forgotten about him and he kept doing the same thing over and over again. Without looking straight at him, out of the corner of my eye I saw that Quimet was looking at the little houses in the distance. Finally he said, "Doesn't that bird scare you?"

I told him I liked the bird, and he said his mother had always told him how birds that were black, even ordinary blackbirds, brought bad luck. All the other times I'd gone out with Quimet, after that first day in the Plaça del Diamant, the first thing he'd asked me, leaning his whole body forward, was whether I'd broken up with Pere yet. And that day he didn't ask and I didn't know how to begin to tell him I'd told Pere it was all over between us. And I felt worried about having said it, because Pere had flamed up like a match when you blow on it. And when I thought about leaving Pere it hurt me inside and the hurt made me realize I'd done something wrong. I was sure of it, because I'd always felt comfortable inside, and when I thought about Pere's face I felt a pain that hurt deep inside me, as if in the middle of the peace I'd felt before a little door had opened that was hiding a nest of scorpions and the scorpions had come out and mixed with the pain and made it sting even more and had swarmed through my blood and made it black. Because Pere, with his voice choked up and his eyes full of tears and shaking, had said I'd wrecked his life. That I'd turned it into a little clot of mud. And while he was looking at the blackbird, Quimet began to talk about Senyor Gaudí. How his father had met Gaudí the day he was run over by a streetcar, how his father had been one of the people who'd taken him to the hospital, poor Senyor Gaudí, such a good person, what a horrible way to die. . . And how there was nothing in the world like Güell Park and the Holy Family Church and the

Pedrera apartment house. I told him that, all in all, there were too many spires and waves. He hit my knee with the edge of his hand and made my leg fly up with surprise and said if I wanted to be his wife I had to start by liking everything he liked. He delivered a long sermon about men and women and the rights of the one and the rights of the other and when I was able to cut in I asked him:

"What if I just can't bring myself to like something?"

"You've got to like it, because that means it's something you don't understand."

And another sermon, very long. He brought up lots of people in his family: his parents, an uncle who had a little chapel and a prayer stool, and Ferdinand and Isabella's mothers who he said were the ones who'd shown the right path.

And then—at first I didn't get the point because he mixed it up with so many other things he was saying—he said, "Poor Maria. . . ." And again Ferdinand and Isabella's mothers and how maybe we could get married soon because he had two friends who were already looking for an apartment for him. And he'd make some furniture that would floor me because he wasn't a carpenter for nothing and he was like Saint Joseph and I was like the Virgin Mary.

He said it all very happily and I was thinking of what he'd meant when he said, "Poor Maria . . ." and my mind was getting further away like the fading light. The blackbird never got tired. He was always popping out on the ground and flying from one tree to another and popping out underneath as if there was a whole flock of blackbirds working on it.

"I'll make a wardrobe for both of us out of bottle-tree

wood, with two compartments. And when the apartment's all furnished, I'll make a little bed for our kid."

He told me he liked children and he didn't, that he'd never been able to make up his mind. The sun was going down and where it no longer reached the shadows were turning blue and it was strange-looking. And Quimet kept talking about different kinds of wood, which one to use, jacaranda or mahogany or oak or holly. . . . It was then—I remember it and I'll always remember it—that he kissed me. And when he started kissing me I saw Our Lord up above in his house inside a puffed-up cloud with bright orange edges that was changing color on one side, and Our Lord spread his arms wide—they were very long—and he grabbed the sides of the cloud and shut himself up in it like it was a cupboard.

"We shouldn't have come today."

And the first kiss faded into another and the whole sky clouded up. I saw a big cloud moving away and other smaller ones come out and they all started following the puffed-up one and Quimet's mouth tasted like coffee and milk. And he shouted, "They're closing!"

"How do you know?"

"Didn't you hear the whistle?"

We got up, startling the blackbird who flew away. The wind whipped up my skirts . . . and we followed the paths downward. There was a girl sitting on a bench made out of ceramic tiles who was picking her nose and rubbing her finger against an eight-point star on the back of the bench. Her dress was the same color as mine and I told Quimet. He didn't answer. When we got to the street I said, "Look, people are still going in . . ." and he said, "Don't worry, they'll throw them out soon." We walked down through the streets and just when I was about to tell him, "You know, Pere and I have broken up," he suddenly stopped and stood in front of me. He took hold of my arms and said, looking at me like there was something weird about me, "Poor Maria."

I was about to tell him not to fret and to tell me what was eating him with this Maria . . . but I didn't dare. Then he let go of my arms and started walking beside me again toward the center of town till we got to the corner of Diagonal and the Passeig de Gràcia. We started walking around the block. My feet were killing me. When we'd been going round and round for half an hour he stopped and took hold of my arms again. We were standing under a streetlight, and just when I was expecting him to say "Poor Maria" again and holding my breath waiting for him to say it, he said angrily:

"If we hadn't gotten out of there so quickly, between the blackbird and everything else, I don't know what would have happened! . . . But don't trust me. The day I catch you I'll hobble you for life."

We walked around the block till it was eight o'clock without saying a word to each other, as if we'd been born mute. When he said goodbye and I was alone again I looked at the sky and it was all black. And I don't know . . . all together, it was very mysterious . . .

I ran into him by surprise standing on the corner one day when he wasn't supposed to pick me up.

"I don't want you working anymore for that boss. I know he's after all the girls in the shop."

I started trembling and told him not to shout, that I couldn't walk out just like that, any old way and as if I hadn't been brought up right, that the poor man hadn't said anything to me that he didn't say to all the others and that I liked selling pastries and that if he tried to make me quit we'd see what . . . He told me how one winter afternoon when it was already dark he'd come to watch me work. And he said that, while I was with a customer who was choosing a box of chocolates in the display case on the right, the boss had followed me with his eyes—not me, my rear end. I told him he was going too far and it'd be better to forget the whole thing if he didn't trust me.

"I do trust you, but I don't like your boss playing around like that."

"You're crazy," I told him. "All he thinks about is his business! You hear me?"

I got so angry my cheeks turned red. He grabbed my neck and shook my head from side to side. I told him to get away from me or I'd call a cop. We didn't see each other for three weeks and when I was wishing I hadn't told Pere everything was over between us, because deep down Pere was a good guy who'd never done anything bad to me, just hard-working and caught up in his job, Quimet turned up again, cool as a cucumber, and the first thing he said, with his hands in his pockets, was "Come on, poor Maria, let's take a walk."

We went down the Rambla del Prat toward the Carrer Gran. He stopped in front of a grocery store with some sacks piled in front of it. He stuck his hand in a sack of birdseed and said, "What nice birdseed. . . ." Then we started walking again. He still had some birdseed in his hand and when I wasn't looking he put it down my neck under my blouse. He made me stop in front of a window full of clothes. "You see? When we're married, I'll send you to buy some smocks like those." I said they'd make me look like an orphan and he said they were like the ones his mother wore and I said I didn't care, they still reminded me of an orphanage.

He said he wanted me to meet his mother, that he'd already told her about me and his mother was very eager to see what kind of girl her son had chosen. We went there one Sunday. She lived alone. Quimet lived in a boarding-house so as not to make more work for her. He said that way they were better friends because they didn't get along well together. His mother lived in a little house down toward the center of town, and from her balcony you could watch the sea and the fog that sometimes hid it. She was a busy little woman who always had a permanent wave. Her house was full of ribbons tied in bows. Quimet had already told me about them. There was a bow above the crucifix at the head of the bed. The bed was made of black mahogany with two mattresses and a cream-colored bedspread with red roses and a wavy red border all around. There was a bow on the night-table key and on all the keys to the dresser drawers. And bows on the keys to all the doors.

"You must like ribbons a lot," I said.

"A house isn't a home without ribbons."

And she asked me if I liked selling pastries and I said, "Yes ma'am, very much, especially curling the ends of the ribbons with a scissors," and how what I looked forward to most was the holidays so I could make lots of packages and hear the cash register ring and the bell above the door.

"You're kidding," she said.

When it was getting on toward evening, Quimet nudged me with his elbow, which meant, "Let's go." And when we were already outside the door his mother asked me, "And you like housework too?"

"Yes ma'am, very much."

"Very good."

Then she told us to wait. She went inside and came back with a rosary with black beads and gave it to me. Quimet, when we'd walked a little way, said I'd won her heart.

"What did she say when you were alone together in the kitchen?"

"That you were a very good boy."

"That's what I thought."

He said it looking at the ground and kicking a pebble. I told him I didn't know what to do with the rosary. He said I should put it in a drawer, that it might come in handy some day and that it was better not to throw anything away.

"Maybe our little girl would like it, if we have one."

And he pinched me under my arm. While I was still rubbing it, because he'd really hurt me, he asked me if I remembered something or other and then he said he was going to buy a motorcycle soon, that it'd come in handy because after we were married we could travel all over the country with me sitting behind him. He asked me if I'd ever ridden behind a man on a motorcycle and I told him no, never, that it looked very scary and he got as happy as a lark and said, "Oh, it's nothing, woman. . . ."

We went to the Monumental Bar to have a vermouth and some baby octopuses. He ran into Cintet, and Cintet, who had very big eyes like a cow and his mouth a little twisted, said there was an apartment for rent on Montseny Street, fairly cheap but run down because the landlord didn't want to be bothered and the new tenants would have to pay to have it fixed up. It was on the top floor. We both liked the idea that it was on the top floor and even more when Cintet told us we'd have the roof all to ourselves. We'd have it to ourselves because the ground-floor tenants had a yard and the people on the second floor had a long outdoor staircase that led to a little garden with a henhouse and a washbasin and Quimet got excited and told Cintet to make sure no one else got it and Cintet said the next day he'd go with Mateu and we should come along too. All of us together. Quimet asked him if he knew about any used motorcycles, because one of Cintet's uncles owned a garage where Cintet worked and Cintet told him he'd keep an eye out. They talked like I wasn't there. My mother had never told me about men. She and my father spent many years quarreling and many more not even speaking to each other. They'd spend Sunday afternoons sitting in the dining room, not saying a word. When my mother died, the silence got even bigger. And when my father remarried a few years later there was nothing left for me to hold onto. I felt the way a cat must feel, running around with his tail between his legs or sticking out. Now it's time to eat, now it's time to sleep. With the difference that a cat doesn't have to work for a living. We lived without words in my house and the things I felt inside scared me because I didn't know where they came from. . . .

When we were saying good-by at the streetcar stop, I heard Cintet say to Quimet, "I don't know where you found such a pretty girl. . . ." And I heard Quimet laughing, "Ha ha ha. . . ."

"I think you're sensible to get married young. You need a husband and a roof over your head."

Senyora Enriqueta, who made her living in the winter selling hot chestnuts and sweet potatoes on the corner in front of the Smart Cinema and selling peanuts and groundnuts during the summer street festivals, always gave me good advice. We'd sit down across from each other, facing her balcony, and she'd pull her sleeves up from time to time. She didn't say anything while she was pulling them up and when she'd finished she'd start talking again. She was tall, with a mouth like a fish and a nose like a paper cone. Summer or winter, she always wore white stockings and black shoes. She had a picture that hung from a yellow ribbon, full of lobsters with gold crowns, with men's faces, and all the grass around the lobsters, who were coming out of a well, was brown, and the sea in the background and the sky up above were the color of cow's blood and the lobsters wore armor and were killing each other with blows from their tails. It was raining outside. The little drops fell on the rooftops, on the streets, on the gardens, on the sea as if it didn't already have enough water, and maybe also on the mountains. It was midafternoon, but we could hardly see. Drops of water hung from the clotheslines and played tag and sometimes one of them would fall and before it fell it would stretch and stretch, because you could see it was hard for it to let go. It had been raining for a week. A fine rain, not too heavy and not too light, and the clouds were so swollen that they drifted right onto the rooftops. We were watching the rain.

"I think Quimet's a better match for you than Pere. He's got his own shop, and Pere has to take orders. Quimet's smarter and has more get up and go."

"But sometimes he sighs and says 'Poor Maria.'"

"But he's going to marry you, right?"

My feet were frozen because my shoes had gotten wet, and the top of my head felt very hot. I told her Quimet wanted to buy a motorcycle and she said you could see he was very modern. And it was Senyora Enriqueta who came with me to buy the material for my wedding gown and when I told her we might get an apartment near her she was very happy.

The apartment was empty. The kitchen stank of cockroaches and I found a nest with long caramel-colored eggs, and Quimet told me, "Keep looking and you'll find more." The dining-room wallpaper had thin circles on it. Quimet said he wanted apple-green wallpaper, and white wallpaper for the child's room with clowns along the edges. And a new kitchen. He asked Cintet to tell Mateu he wanted to see him. Next Sunday afternoon we all went to the apartment. Mateu immediately started tearing the kitchen apart, and the bricklayer, his pants all covered with bits of plaster, carried the rubble downstairs and loaded it in a handcart he had in the street. But the bricklayer made a mess on the stairs and a woman on the second floor came out and told him we'd better not leave without cleaning up because she didn't want to slip and break her neck. . . . And Quimet said from time to time: "I hope no one's stealing the handcart. . . ." We and Cintet began wetting down the dining-room walls, and then we started scraping off the wallpaper. After we'd been working for a while, we noticed that Quimet wasn't there. Cintet said Quimet was as slippery as an eel when there was something he didn't feel like doing. I went in the kitchen to get a drink of water. The back of Mateu's shirt was soaked and his face was shining with sweat and he never stopped pounding on the chisel with his hammer.

I went back to scraping wallpaper. And Cintet said when Quimet came back he'd act like nothing had happened and he was sure he'd come back late. It was hard to get the paper unstuck, and under the first layer we found another and another till there were five altogether. When it was dark and we were washing up Quimet came back. He said while he'd been helping the bricklayer put the rubble in the handcart one of his clients had come along. . . . And Cintet said, "And of course you spent some time with him. . . ." And Quimet without looking at him said there was more work than he'd realized but that we'd get it all done. When we were going downstairs Mateu said they were going to make me a kitchen fit for a queen. And then Quimet wanted to go up on the roof. There was a breeze blowing and you could see lots of rooftops, but the bay window on the second floor blocked our view of the street. And we left. Between our landing and the second floor the wall was covered with names and drawings. And among the names and drawings there were some very well-drawn scales, with the lines carved into the wall like they'd been made with an icepick. One side of the scales hung down a little lower than the other. I ran my finger along one of them. We went to have vermouth and some baby octopuses. Halfway through the week I quarreled again with Quimet because of his obsession with my boss.

"If I see him looking at your rear end again like that, I'll come in and he'll hear about it!" he shouted. He disappeared for two or three days, and when he came back and I asked him if he'd calmed down he got madder than a wet hen and said he'd come to demand an explanation because he'd seen me in the street with Pere. I told him he must have made a mistake. He said he'd seen me. I swore it wasn't so and he swore it was. At first I spoke calmly, but since he wouldn't believe me he made me start yelling and when he saw I was yelling he said all women were crazy and they weren't worth a nickel and I asked him where he'd seen me with Pere.

"In the street."

"What street?"

"In the street."

"What street? What street?"

He stormed off. I didn't sleep all night. The next day he came back and told me I had to promise not to go out with Pere and to put an end to it and not hear his voice anymore, which didn't sound like his own when he was mad, I told him I'd do as he said and not go out with Pere anymore. Instead of calming down he got madder than a devil. He told me he was fed up with my lies, that he'd set a trap for me and I'd been caught in it like a mouse, and he made me apologize for taking a walk with Pere and then telling him I hadn't and in the end he got me to the point where I believed I *had* gone out with Pere and he told me to kneel down.

"In the middle of the street?"

"Then kneel down inwardly."

And he made me apologize, kneeling down inwardly, for having gone for a walk with Pere who, poor me, I hadn't seen since we'd broken up. The next Sunday I went to help scrape the wallpaper. Quimet didn't come till it was time to stop because he had to work on some furniture he was making. Mateu had almost finished the kitchen. One more afternoon and he'd be done. He'd put white tiles along the bottom of the walls up to about a yard from the floor. And bright red tiles above the stove. Mateu said the tiles were from where he worked. And that it was his wedding present. He and Quimet hugged each other while Cintet, with a dull look in his cow's-eyes, washed his hands. We all went out together to have a vermouth and some baby octopuses. Cintet said if we needed a ring he knew a jeweler who'd give it to us at the best price. And Mateu said he knew one who'd give it to us half price.

"I don't know how you do it," Quimet told him.

And Mateu, blond and blue-eyed, laughed happily and looked at us slowly, first one and then the other.

"He's a smart guy."

The night before Palm Sunday my father asked me when we were planning to get married. He was walking into the dining room ahead of me, with the outsides of his heels worn away. I told him we didn't know. . . . when the apartment was ready.

"Is there much left to do?"

I told him I wasn't sure because it depended on how much time we could put into it. That there were at least five layers of wallpaper and Quimet wanted to get them all off because he wanted everything just right so it would last the rest of our lives.

"Have him come for dinner Sunday."

When I told Quimet about it he exploded.

"I went to ask him for your hand and he acted like he

couldn't care less and said I was the third one and we'd see if I was the last, just to make me hurry up. And now he invites me to dinner? Once we're married . . ."

We went to see them bless the palms. There were boys and girls with woven palm leaves and boys and girls with noisemakers and some had wooden maces instead of noisemakers and were killing Jews on the walls and on the ground and on top of metal drums and water barrels and everywhere. When we got to Saint Joseph's Church everyone started shouting. Mateu came with us, carrying his little girl on his shoulders, as pretty as a flower. She had long blonde curls and her eyes were blue like Mateu's, but she never laughed. She was carrying a woven palm branch that Mateu helped her hold up, all covered with glazed cherries. Another father had a little boy on his shoulders and was holding a little palm branch with a blue silk bow and a diamond cross and the two fathers, pushed forward by the crowd and without noticing, got closer and closer and the little boy started picking the cherries off Mateu's daughter's palm and by the time we noticed he'd stripped half of one side.

We went to Quimet's mother's house for dinner. She had a bunch of little boxwood branches on the table, tied together with a little red ribbon. And little palm leaves tied with a red ribbon because I'd told her I was going to see the palms blessed. And a woman came in from the garden and Quimet's mother introduced her to us. She was a neighbor Quimet's mother had taken in because she'd quarreled with her husband.

When it was dinnertime and we'd already started eating, Quimet asked for the salt. His mother looked up quickly and said he always put too much salt on his food. And Quimet said, "It's too bland today." The neighbor said she didn't think it was either bland or salty; just right. And Quimet said it was as bland as could be. His mother stood up very straight and went into the kitchen and came back with a saltshaker shaped like a rabbit so the salt came out of its ears. She left the saltshaker on the table and said in a very cold voice: "The salt." And Quimet, instead of putting some salt on his food, started saying what if we were all made of salt ever since that lady who didn't believe her husband and who suddenly turned around when he'd told her to walk straight ahead. Quimet's mother told him to shut up and eat, and he asked the neighbor if he was right or wrong when he said the lady shouldn't have turned around and the neighbor, still chewing and swallowing her food very politely, said she was sure she didn't know anything about it.

And then Quimet said, "The devil," and when he said "The devil" his voice got lower and, speaking to his mother while he sprinkled salt on his food with the rabbit-saltshaker, he said, "Look. You see? Not a grain of salt. You spent all morning tying little bows and not a grain of salt." And I stuck up for Quimet's mother and said yes, she had put salt in the food. And the neighbor said if she ate food that was too salty it took her appetite away and Quimet said now he understood, that his mother had cooked the food without salt for her sake but that it was one thing to cook a dinner for some neighbor and another to try and convince her son that she'd put salt in it when she hadn't. And that everyone knew the devil . . . and his mother told him to stop being such a pest but he went on like he hadn't heard her, saying the devil had created diabetics who were made of sugar just in order to bother people. "We're all made of salt: our sweat, our tears . . ." and he said to me, "Lick your hand and you'll see what it tastes like." And then the devil again, and the neighbor said he was like a child believing in the devil, and Quimet said, "The devil" again and his mother said, "Shut up." And Quimet still hadn't touched his food and we were all half finished and that was when he said the devil was God's shadow and he was everywhere too, in the plants, in the mountains, in the street, inside people's houses, above and below the ground, and how he went around disguised as a big black horsefly with red and blue blood and when he was only a horsefly he stuffed himself full of garbage and half-rotten dead animals thrown on dungheaps. And he pushed his plate away and said he wasn't hungry anymore and he'd just have dessert.

The next Sunday he came to dinner at my house and brought my father a cigar. I bought a long cake filled with custard. All through the meal Quimet talked about different kinds of wood and how hard or soft they were. When we were having coffee Quimet asked me if I wanted to leave or stay a while longer and I said I didn't care. But my stepmother said it was better for young people to go out and have a good time and at three we were out on the street with the sun beating down on us. We went to the apartment to scrape wallpaper. Cintet was already there. He'd brought two rollers and was looking at them with Mateu. Mateu said he knew a paperhanger who'd paper the walls for free if Quimet gave him some legs for a table he had where they were all worm-eaten and it was falling apart because when his children were at home alone they'd bounce it up and down deliberately to make it fall apart. And they agreed to do it.

And when the dining room was papered, a spot appeared on the right. They made the paperhanger come back and he said it wasn't his fault, that the stain must have appeared afterwards. That there was something wrong with the wall and a pipe must have burst inside it. And Quimet said the stain must have already been there and that he should have told us there was a wet spot. Mateu said the best thing was to go see the neighbors because maybe they had their sink on that side and if there was a leak from it we were done for. All three of them went next door. The neighbors weren't very friendly. They said maybe we had a stain but they didn't and they gave Quimet their landlord's address. The landlord said he'd send someone to look at it but no one came and finally he came in person, took a good look at the stain, and said we or our landlord would have to pay for it because we'd made it chipping at the walls. Quimet told him we hadn't chipped at anything. The landlord said it came from when we'd redone the kitchen and he washed his hands of it. Quimet got so mad he almost rose off the ground. Mateu said if it had to be fixed the best thing was to split the cost. But the neighbors' landlord didn't want to hear anything about it. "Go see your own landlord," he said.

"If the stain's coming from your side, what good will it do to go see our landlord?" And the neighbors' landlord said the stain couldn't be coming from his side and he could prove there was nothing on his side that could cause a stain. The landlord went away and everyone started pacing up and down. And all together, it was just so much walking around, so much talking and getting mad for nothing, for something not worth the trouble, for something that finally went away when we put the sideboard in front of it.

Every Sunday we went to the Monumental to have a vermouth and some baby octopuses. One day a man in a yellow shirt came up to us trying to sell postcards of a singer who'd been the queen of Paris many years ago. He said he was her agent and that the singer, who'd been the mistress of kings and princes, now lived by selling her possessions and souvenirs. Quimet yelled at him to get away. When we left he said I should go home because he had an appointment with a gentleman who wanted three bedrooms renovated. I wandered around a little on the Carrer Gran looking in the shop windows. And the window with the dolls in the oilcloth shop. Some creeps started saying things to annoy me and one who looked like a gypsy came closer than the others and said, "Wow, what a dish!" Like I was a bowl of soup. All together, I didn't think it was very funny. It's true, though, that my father always said I was touchy . . . but I really didn't have any idea what I was doing in the world.

He said he'd take me to meet Father Joan. And while we were on our way he told me we had to go fifty-fifty on the apartment. Like we were just friends. I got yelled at for it at home because my father took care of the little bit of money I had left over after his wife had taken some out for food. Finally my father said yes, he'd pay half the rent. But Quimet told me all that stuff about the rent while we were going to see Father Joan.

Father Joan seemed made of flies' wings. I mean his clothes. A kind of shiny black. He received us like a saint. Quimet started telling him, "To me, this marriage business—is just a moment, and the less it costs the better and if we can do it in five minutes instead of ten that's fine." Father Joan, who'd known Quimet since he was little, spread his hands on his knees, leaned forward, and with his eyes a little bleary, because you could see the years had gotten to his eyes, said, "Don't you believe it. Marriage is something that lasts a lifetime, and you have to treat it with respect. You get dressed up on Sunday, don't you? Well, a wedding is like a big Sunday. It needs ceremony. If people didn't respect anything, it'd be like we were still savages. And you don't want to be a savage, do you?" Quimet listened to him with his head down, and when he started to say something, Father Joan motioned him to be quiet.

"I'll marry you, and I think it's better if you do it calmly. I know young people are high-spirited. They want to live and live fast . . . but a life, if it's really going to be a life, has to be lived slowly. I bet your fiancée would rather wear a wedding gown and have everyone who sees her know she's a bride than wear an everyday dress even if it's a nice one. . . . Women are like that. And in all the marriages I've performed—all the good ones, that is—the bride wore a wedding gown."

When we left, Quimet said, "I have a lot of respect for him because he's a good man."

The only thing I took from my house was the brass bed, which was the only thing that was mine. Cintet gave us a metal dining-room lamp with a strawberry-colored silk fringe. The lamp hung from the ceiling on three metal chains that were joined together by a metal flower with three petals. My wedding gown came down to the floor. Quimet wore a dark suit. The apprentice came, and so did Cintet's family: three sisters and two married brothers with their wives. My father was there to lead me to the altar; and Quimet's mother in a black silk dress that crackled every time she moved. All together we made quite a crowd. Mateu's wife, whose name was Griselda, couldn't come because at the last minute she didn't feel well and Mateu said it happened a lot and we'd have to excuse her.

Everything took a long time and Father Joan gave a lovely sermon. He talked about Adam and Eve, the apple and the serpent, and told how woman was made from man's rib and how Adam had found her sleeping beside him without Our Lord having prepared him for the surprise. He told us what Paradise was like: with streams and lawns and sky-blue flowers, and how when Eve woke up the first thing she did was take a blue flower and blow on it and the petals fluttered for a moment and Adam scolded her because she'd hurt the flower. Because Adam, who was the father of all men, desired only the good. And how everything ended with the flaming sword. . . . "It sure turned out lousy," said Senyora Enriqueta, who was sitting behind me, and I wondered what Father Joan would have said if he'd seen that picture of the lobsters with such weird heads, killing each other with their tails . . .

Everyone said the sermon was one of the nicest Father Joan had ever given and the apprentice told Quimet's mother how Father Joan had talked about Paradise and our first ancestors and the angel and the flaming sword at his sister's wedding, too—everything the same. The only difference was the flowers, which he'd said were yellow at his sister's wedding, and the water in the stream, which he'd said was blue in the morning and pink in the afternoon.

We went to the sacristy to sign the papers and then the cars took us to Montjüich Park so we could walk around and work up an appetite. And when we'd walked for a while and our guests were having a vermouth, Quimet and I went to have our picture taken. They took several shots: with Quimet sitting and me standing and with Quimet standing and me sitting. And with both of us sitting with our backs half turned and another with us sitting facing each other, "So it won't look like you're always quarreling," the photographer said. And another of us standing side by side, me with my hand on a low three-legged table that kept wobbling and another with the two of us sitting on a bench next to a tree made of tulle and paper.

When we got to the Monumental they said they'd gotten tired of waiting for us and we told them the photographer had taken some very artistic shots and that took time. In any case, there were no more olives and anchovies left and Quimet said it didn't matter and we should start lunch, but he felt he should tell them they had bad manners. And he spent the whole time arguing with Cintet, the olives this and the olives that. Mateu didn't say anything, but he looked at me from time to time and chuckled. And he leaned over behind my father's chair and said, "They're always good for a laugh." The meal was delicious, and when we'd finished they put on some records and everyone danced. My father danced with me. At first I danced with my veil on but in the end I took it off and gave it to Senyora Enriqueta so I could dance better. And when I danced I held my dress up because I was afraid I'd step on it and I danced a waltz with Mateu and he danced well and swept me along like a feather, like I'd been dancing all my life, he led so well. I was blushing. I danced with the apprentice, who wasn't very good at it, and Quimet laughed at him to make him angry but the apprentice went right on as if he hadn't noticed.

And halfway through the dancing four gentlemen came in who'd been eating in the next room and asked if they could join us. They were all old, at least in their forties. And after those four, two more came in. A half-dozen all together. And they said they were celebrating the removal of the youngest one's appendix. He had a little cord hanging from his ear because he was hard of hearing. They said we could see the operation had gone very well and they'd been told there was a wedding dance next door and they thought they'd see if we'd let them join in because they needed some joy and youthfulness. And all the gentlemen congratulated me and asked me who was the groom and gave him cigars and they danced with me and everyone was full of laughter.

When he saw those gentlemen who were celebrating the operation with us, the waiter who was serving liqueurs asked if he could have one dance with the bride, that it was a custom of his and it brought him good luck. He said if we didn't mind he'd write my name in a notebook where he kept the names of all the brides he'd danced with, and he wrote my name down and showed us the notebook which had seven pages full of names. He was as thin as an asparagus stalk, with rather sunken cheeks and only one tooth. He wore his hair all combed to one side to cover his bald spot. The waiter said he felt like dancing a waltz, but Quimet decided to put on a very fast two-step and the waiter and I were like two arrows shooting forwards and backwards and everyone was very happy and in the middle Quimet said he wanted to finish the two-step with me because he'd met me dancing a two-step, and the waiter gave me back to Quimet and then smoothed his hair down to make sure his bald spot wasn't showing, but instead he messed it up even more and his hair went in all directions. The gentlemen from the operation were all standing by the door. They were dressed in black with white carnations in their lapels, and while I was dancing I saw them on a slant and they seemed from another world. While we were dancing Quimet said what made them think they could make a fool of him, that the only thing missing was Father Joan with his sermon to spoil our fun. Everyone clapped and I couldn't breathe and my heart was pounding and that was where the joy started that you could see in my eyes. And when it was over I wished it was the day before so we could start all over again, it was so lovely. . . .

We'd been married for two months and a week. Quimet's mother had given us a mattress and we'd gotten an old-fashioned bedspread with flowers crocheted on it from Senyora Enriqueta. The mattress cover was blue, with a pattern of curly feathers that shined. The bed was made of light-colored wood. The headboard and legs had rows of little columns and the columns were made of balls, one on top of the other. The bed was high enough so you could easily get under it. I found that out by experience the first day I put on a chestnut colored dress I'd made with a very elegant cream collar. The skirt was all pleated and had little gold buttons down the front. After we'd eaten supper, without saying anything so I could surprise him, while Quimet was sketching a piece of furniture under the metal lamp that made a ring of light on the table, I went to put on my new dress and when I had it on I came back into the dining room. Without raising his head from his work, Quimet asked me:

"What were you doing so quietly?"

He looked at me, and the shadow of the strawberry-colored fringe fell on half his face and it was days since he'd said, "We'll have to hang that lamp higher so it casts more light." I stood in front of him and he looked at me and didn't say even half a word and he stayed like that for quite a while and I couldn't stand it anymore and he kept on looking at me. In the shadow his eyes looked even smaller and more sunken and just when I felt like I couldn't stand it a minute longer he jumped up like a jet of water from a fountain, with his arms raised and his fingers spread so wide I thought the skin between them was going to burst and he threw himself on me going, "Oooooo, oooooo . . ." I started running down the hall with Quimet behind me going "Oooooo . . . Oooooo. . . ." I made it to the bedroom and he followed me in and threw me on the floor and pushed me under the bed with his feet and jumped on top of the bed. When I tried to get out he'd slap my head from above. "Bad girl!" he shouted. And no matter where I tried to get out, whack! his hand would hit my head. "Bad girl!" From then on he played that joke a lot.

One day I saw some very pretty hot-chocolate cups and I bought six of them: all white. And when Quimet saw them he got mad: "What are we going to do with those hot-chocolate cups?"

At that moment Cintet showed up, and without even asking how we were he told us a friend of Mateu's knew a man on Bertran Street who wanted all the furniture in his house restored. "He says you should be there tomorrow at one. It's a three-story house. You can make back everything you spent getting married, because he's in a hurry and you'll be able to charge overtime." Quimet wrote down the address and then he opened the kitchen cupboard. "You can see how we waste our time. Neither of us likes hot chocolate. It's as dumb as cleaning a cat's fur for him . . ." Cintet laughed and picked up one of the cups and pretended to drink from it and put it back next to the others. They knew I didn't like hot chocolate.

With what he made restoring the man on Bertran Street's furniture, he bought a used motorcycle. It had belonged to a man who'd died in an accident and they hadn't found his corpse until the next day. We'd roar down the highways on the motorcycle, making the chickens squawk and scaring the people.

"Hold on tight. This is going to be a nice one."

What worried me most were the turns. We'd be almost flat against the ground and, when the road straightened out, we'd be upright again. "When you met me did you ever think I'd make you eat kilometers?" On the curves my face would freeze and get as stiff as a board. Tears would come to my eyes, and with my cheek against Quimet's back, I'd be thinking all the time that I'd never get home alive.

"Today we'll go along the coast."

We had lunch in Badalona. We didn't get farther than Badalona because we'd gotten up too late. The sea didn't seem like water; the clouds had made it gray and sad. And the swelling that came from inside was the fish breathing and their anger was the sea's breath when it rose higher and made waves and bubbles. While we were having coffee, like a treacherous dagger, "Poor Maria" again.

My nose started bleeding and I couldn't stop it. I put a

penny between my eyes. I put the front door key, which was very big, behind my neck. The waiter in the café went with me to the bathroom and helped me splash some water on my head. When I came back Quimet's lips were pursed and his nose was red with anger. "Wait till it's time to leave a tip. Then he'll see who he's dealing with. Not a cent."

He said the waiter shouldn't have gone with me and I asked him why he hadn't come himself and he said I was big enough to go alone. When he'd gotten on the motorcycle, he started in again: "If Maria could see these hundred horsepower . . ."

I began to take it seriously. A few days before he was going to say "Poor Maria" I'd know it was coming because his mind would wander. And after he'd said it and he saw I was upset he'd get very quiet like I wasn't there, but I could feel him relaxing inside. And I couldn't get Maria out of my head. If I was washing dishes I'd think, "Maria probably gets them cleaner." If I was making the bed I'd think, "Maria probably tucks the sheets in tighter. . . ." And all I thought about was Maria, day in and day out. I hid the cups. When I thought of how I'd bought them without Quimet's permission, my heart would freeze. And whenever Quimet's mother saw me, she'd ask, "Any news?"

And Quimet, with his arms flat against his sides and his hands spread palms outward, would shrug his shoulders and not say a word. But I could hear what he was saying inside and he was saying, "It's not my fault." And his mother would look at me with a glazed look in her eyes: "Maybe she doesn't eat enough. . . ." She'd touch my arms. "She's not *that* skinny."

"She's tricky," said Quimet, and he looked at both of us.

Whenever we went there, his mother would always say she'd made us a hundred-dollar meal. And when we left Quimet always said, "What do you think of my mother's cooking?" And we'd get on the motorcycle. Rruuum . . . Rruuum. Like thunder. Those nights, when I was getting undressed, I knew it was coming. "Since it's Sunday, today we'll make a child." The next morning he'd jump out of bed like a whirlwind and throw back the blankets without looking to see if he was uncovering me. He'd go out on the balcony and take deep breaths. Then he'd make a big racket washing up and come into the dining room singing. He'd sit down at the table and wind his legs around the legs of the chair. I still hadn't seen his shop and one day he told me to come along. The paint had been scraped off the windows but the panes were so dirty you couldn't see in or out. When I told him I'd wash the windows he said, "Don't mess with the shop." There were some very pretty tools and two pots of glue, a dry glue that trickled down the sides of the pots, and when I touched the stick inside one of them he slapped my hand and said, "Now, now. Don't make a mess."

And he introduced me to his apprentice as if we'd never met. "My wife, Colometa." The apprentice, with his crafty child's face, offered me his hand. "Andreuet, at your service."

And always the same thing. "Colometa, Colometa . . ." And his mother: "Any news?" And the day I said too much food on my plate made me sick and would she please take a little back, Quimet's mother said, "It's about time." She made me go into the bedroom. There were bows on the posts of that black bed with the red roses on the bedspread: a blue bow, a lavender bow, a yellow bow, and an orange one. She made me lie down. She touched me and listened to me like a doctor. "Not yet," she said when we came back into the dining room. And Quimet, flicking his cigar ash on the floor, said he'd thought so.

And he made the chair. He'd been working on the plans at night for a long time, coming to bed when I was already asleep. He'd wake me up and tell me the hardest part was finding the balance point. He'd discuss it with Cintet and Mateu on Sundays when the weather was bad and we stayed at home. It was very strange: part regular chair, part rocking chair, and part armchair. It took him a long time to make it. He said it was Majorcan style. All wood. It only rocked a little. And he said I'd have to make a cushion the same color as the fringe on the lamp. Two of them: one for the seat and one for a headrest. He was the only one who could sit in the chair.

"It's a man's chair," he said. And I left it at that. He added that we'd have to polish it every Sunday so all the juice would come out of the wood and make it shine. He'd sit in the chair and cross his legs. If he was smoking, he'd blow the smoke out with his eyes half shut, like some kind of sweetness was going all through him. I told Senyora Enriqueta about it.

"Well, it doesn't do him any harm, does it? It's better for him to have fun sitting down than riding around like a madman on that motorcycle."

And she told me to watch myself with Quimet's mother and especially never to let Quimet know what I was thinking, because if he was the type who enjoyed making people suffer, it was better he didn't know my weak points. I told her I was fond of Quimet's mother—the poor woman—because of that funny mania she had for making bows. But Senyora Enriqueta said that the bow business was just an act the woman put on to make people think she was dumb. That in any case, I had to make her think I loved her, because Quimet would be satisfied with me if his mother liked me.

On Sundays when we didn't go out because it was raining and Mateu and Cintet didn't come over, we'd spend the afternoon in bed, with those columns of honey-colored wooden balls one on top of the other. While we were having lunch he'd announce:

"Today we'll make a child."

And I'd see stars. Senyora Enriqueta had been hinting for a while that she'd like to hear about our wedding night. But I didn't dare tell her because we didn't have a wedding night. We had a wedding week. Up to the moment he got undressed, you could say I'd never really taken a good look at him. I was sitting in a corner, too nervous to move, and finally he said, "If you're embarrassed to get undressed in front of me I'll leave the room, and if you're not, I'll go first so you can see it's no big deal." His hair was bushy as a jungle and as shiny as patent leather. He combed it with rough strokes and at each stroke of the comb he'd run his fingers through it quickly, as if one hand was chasing the other. When he didn't comb it one lock would come down over his forehead, which was broad and rather low. His eyebrows were thick, black like his hair, set above his bright little monkey eyes. His eyelids were always shiny, as if someone had oiled them, and it made him look handsome. His nose wasn't too wide or too narrow or turned up, which I wouldn't have liked at all. His cheeks were full, pink in the summer and red in the winter. His ears on each side seemed a little disconnected from the part above them. And his lips were always bright and rather big, with the lower one sticking out. When he talked or laughed, you could see all his teeth lined up, each one firmly planted in the gum. His neck was smooth. And in his nose—which like I said wasn't too wide or too narrow—he had a little grille of hairs in each nostil to keep out the cold and the dust. Sometimes the veins would swell up like snakes on the backs of his legs, which were on the thin side. His whole body was long, and rounded where it should be. His chest was broad and his ankles were thin. His feet were long and slender with slightly fallen arches, and when he walked around barefoot you could hear his feet slapping against the floor. He was pretty well-built and I told him so, and he walked around the room slowly and asked me, "You think so?"

I felt terrified in my corner. And when he'd gotten into bed, to set an example as he said, I started to get undressed. I'd always been afraid of that moment. They'd told me the path leading to it was strewn with flowers and the one going away was strewn with tears. And that joy leads to disillusionment. Because when I was little I'd heard people say they rip you open. And I'd always been scared it would kill me. They said women die ripped open. It begins when they get married. And if they're still not broken, the midwife finishes them off with a knife or a piece of broken bottle. And you stay that way forever, either ripped open or sewn up, and that's why married women get tired quicker when they have to stay on their feet for a while. And when there are women standing in a crowded streetcar, the men who know about it get up and give them their seats and the men who don't know about it stay seated.

And when I started crying Quimet raised his head above the sheets and asked me what was the matter and I told him the truth: I was scared of dying ripped apart. And he laughed and said yes, there had been one case: Queen Bustamante, whose husband, to avoid trouble, had had her opened up by a horse and she'd died as a result. And he laughed and laughed and laughed. That's why I couldn't tell Senyora Enriqueta about our wedding night, because the day we were married, when we got back to the apartment, Quimet sent me out to buy food, barred the door, and made our wedding night last a week. But I did tell Senyora Enriqueta about the case of Queen Bustamante and she said yes it was horrible, but not as horrible as what her husband had done to her. He'd been dead and buried now for years, with the rain watering him and the mallow roses growing on top of him. He'd crucified her, tying her to the bed because she was always trying to run away. And when she insisted on hearing about my wedding night I managed to distract her, and one good distraction was the rocking chair. And another was the story about the lost key.

One night, after we'd left the Monumental Bar, we walked around with Cintet till two in the morning. and when we got home and Cintet was about to leave, we couldn't get in. The front door key had disappeared. Quimet said he'd given it to me so I could keep it in my purse. Cintet, who'd had supper at our house, said he thought he'd seen Quimet take it off the nail behind the door, which was where we always kept it, and that he'd put it in his pocket. Quimet looked in all his pockets to see if there were any holes in them. I said maybe he'd told Cintet someone should take the downstairs key and Cintet, without noticing, had taken it and didn't remember and he was the one who'd lost it. Then they said I'd taken it but they couldn't remember when or if they'd seen me. Cintet said, "Ring the second-floor bell." Quimet didn't want to and he was right. It was better not to have anything to do with the people on the second floor. Finally Quimet said, "It's lucky the shop's so near. Let's go get some tools."

Both of them went to look for tools to open the door. I stayed in the doorway to see if the night watchman would come along, because I'd called him by clapping my hands on the corner and he hadn't come and there was no sign of him anywhere. I got tired of standing up and sat down on the front step. With my head against the door, I watched the patch of sky between the buildings. There was a light breeze blowing, and the sky was very dark with scurrying clouds. I had to make a great effort not to close my eyes. I was getting very sleepy. And the night, the breeze, and those passing clouds, all blown in the same direction, made me sleepy and I wondered what Quimet and Cintet would say if they came back and found me curled up asleep in front of the door, so sound asleep I couldn't even get up the stairs. . . . In the distance I could already hear their steps on the sidewalk.

Quimet drilled a hole in the door just above the lock. Cintet kept saying it was illegal and Quimet kept saying he'd plug the hole but he had to get into his house. And when he'd drilled a hole all the way through the wood, he made a wire hook and fished around for the cord—the door opened by pulling a cord—and he got it open just as the night watchman came around the corner. We slipped in as fast as we could and Cintet got away. When we got into the apartment the first thing we saw was the key hanging behind the door. The next day Quimet plugged the hole with cork and if anyone knew what had happened, they didn't say anything. "So you didn't lose the key," Senyora Enriqueta said. And I told her, "As long as we thought we'd lost it, it was like we had lost it."

And it came time for the neighborhood street festival. Quimet said we'd dance in the Plaça del Diamant and that we'd dance the last dance together. We spent the week of the festival cooped up in our apartment. Quimet was furious because he'd done some restoration that had been a lot of work, and the man who'd asked him to do it turned out to be a Jew and had gypped him, and Quimet, to get it over with, had taken what he could get but he'd lost money. And I had to pay for his bad mood. And when he was in a bad mood he'd start in with "Colometa, get a move on," "Colometa, look what a mess you made," "Come here, Colometa," "Go over there, Colometa," "So calm, how can you always be so calm? . . . " And he paced up and down like a caged beast. He opened all the drawers and threw everything on the floor and when I asked him what he was looking for he didn't say anything. He was furious that I wasn't mad at the man who'd cheated him. And since I didn't want to get mad, I left him alone. I combed my hair and when I was opening the door to go out for something to drink because cleaning up his mess had made me thirsty, he stopped acting so crazy. The whole street was glittering with joy and pretty girls in pretty dresses went by and some people threw down a shower of confetti from their balcony, all different colors, and I tucked a few pieces into my hair so they'd stay there.

I came back with two bottles. Quimet was sitting in his chair half asleep. The streets glittering with joy and me picking clothes up off the floor and folding them and putting them away. And later in the afternoon we went to his mother's house on the motorcycle to say hello.

"Are you getting along well?"

"Yes, ma'am."

When we'd left and Quimet was kicking the starter, he asked me, "What were you two whispering about together?"

I said I'd been telling his mother he'd gotten a lot of work and he told me I'd made a mistake because his mother was a spendthrift and for a while she'd been after him to buy her a feather duster and a new gray-and-white mattress cover. And one day Quimet's mother told me how stubborn he was and how he'd driven her crazy when he was little. How when she told him to do something and he didn't want to he'd sit down on the floor and wouldn't get up till she'd practically brained him by hitting his head.

And one Sunday morning Quimet started complaining about his leg. He said his leg hurt while he was asleep, and it felt like the marrow in his bones was on fire, or sometimes the place between the flesh and the bone. And that he never felt the fire in his marrow and between the flesh and bone at the same time, that when he felt it in the marrow he didn't feel it between the flesh and bone. "When I put my feet on the ground it goes away."

"Which bone?"

"Which bone? All of them! A little bit in my calf bone and a little bit in my thighbone but my knee's okay." He said maybe it was rheumatism. Senyora Enriqueta said she didn't believe it, that he was just saying it to get attention. All winter he complained about his leg. And in the morning he'd explain to me very precisely, with his eyes barely open and while he was eating breakfast, everything his leg had done to him during the night. His mother said, "Colometa should put hot towels on it." And he said they'd make it hurt more and it hurt enough already. As soon as I saw him come in, at lunchtime or in the evening, I'd ask him how his leg was, and he'd say that some days it didn't bother him.

He'd lie down on the bed. He'd fall onto it like a sack and I was always terrified he'd break the springs. He wanted me to take his shoes off and put on his checkered coffee-and-milk-colored slippers. After he'd rested a while he'd come to supper. Before going to sleep he'd ask me to rub his whole body with alcohol, for the pain he said. His whole body, because he said the pain was tricky and it'd move up or down if I left some parts alone.

I told everyone it only hurt at night, and everyone said it was very strange. And the lady in the grocery store downstairs thought it was strange too. "That leg still won't let him sleep?" "How's your husband's leg?" "Very well, thanks. It only hurts at night." "Does his leg still hurt?" his mother would ask.

One day on the Rambla with the flower stalls, in the midst of a storm of smells and colors, I heard a voice behind me.

"Natalia . . ."

I thought of how used I was to only hearing, "Colometa, Colometa." It was my first fiancé, Pere. The one I'd left. I was afraid to ask him if he'd gotten married or was engaged. We shook hands and his lower lip trembled a little. He told me he'd been left alone in the world. Till then I hadn't noticed he was wearing a black armband. And he gazed at me like he was drowning in the crowd, in the flowers, among all those stalls. He told me how one day he'd run into Julieta and Julieta had told him I was married and as soon as he heard it he thought of how much he wished me luck. I lowered my eyes because I didn't know what to say or do, and I felt like I had to roll the sadness into a ball, a bullet, a bit of grapeshot. Swallow it. And since he was taller than me, while I was standing with my head down I felt the weight of all the sadness Pere carried inside him on top of my head and it seemed like he saw everything inside me, all my secrets and my pain. And thank God there were all those flowers.

When Quimet came home for lunch, the first thing I told him was that I'd run into Pere.

"Pere?" and he twisted up his mouth. "I don't know who you're talking about."

"The guy I left to marry you."

"You didn't speak to him, did you?"

I told him we'd asked each other how we were, and he said I should have acted like I didn't know him. And I told him Pere had said he barely recognized me and that he'd had to look and look before calling out, because I'd gotten so thin.

"Let him worry about himself."

And I didn't tell him that when I got off the streetcar I'd gone to look at the dolls in the window of the oilcloth shop and that's why lunch was late.

Quimet's mother made the sign of the cross on my forehead and wouldn't let me dry the dishes. I was pregnant. When she'd washed the dishes she closed the kitchen door. We went and sat down on the back porch covered with grapevines at one end and Saint-John's-wort at the other. Quimet said he was sleepy and left us by ourselves. That was when Quimet's mother told me what Quimet and Cintet had done to her when they were small and Cintet spent every Thursday afternoon at their house. She told me she'd planted three dozen jonquils and every morning, as soon as she got up, she'd go see how they were growing. She said jonquils came out of their bulbs very slowly so people would long for them more and that in the end the stems would be covered with processions of little buds. And from the buds you could guess what color the flowers were going to be. There was more pink than anything else. And one Thursday afternoon the two boys were playing in the garden and when she came out to bring them their tea she suddenly saw all the jonquils planted upside down: each stem with four hairy little roots sticking up. And all the buds, the leaves, and the stems buried. She told me she said just one word, even though she'd never been one to swear, and she wouldn't tell me what that word was. And she said, "Little boys can make you suffer a lot. If it's a boy, be careful."

When my father found out I was pregnant—Quimet had gone over to tell him—he came to see me and said that whether it was a boy or a girl his name was finished. Senyora Enriqueta kept asking me if I felt any desire.

"If you feel the urge, don't touch yourself. And if you do, touch yourself from behind."

She told me some very nasty stories about cravings people get: for raisins, for cherries, for liver. The worst craving of all was for kid's head. She'd known a woman who'd had a craving for kid's head. And Senyora Enriqueta had seen the woman's craving on her child's cheek, with little shadows of the kid's eye and ear. And then she told me how babies take shape in the fluid: first their hearts, then gradually their nerves and veins and then the backbone and gristle, because otherwise we wouldn't fit inside our mothers' wombs, since we have to be curled up there. How if the womb was longer we'd be able to stand up in it and our backbones would be straight as broomsticks. And even when we were small we wouldn't be able to bend over.

When summer came, the midwife said I needed lots of fresh air and swimming. So out came the motorcycle and off we went to the beach. We took everything we needed: food and clothing. We used a yellow-and-blue-and-black-striped towel as a curtain. Quimet held it stretched out full length so I could get undressed behind it. He laughed at me, because you could see I looked funny with a belly that wasn't mine. And I watched the waves come in and go out, always the same, always the same—all of them in a hurry to get there and in a hurry to get away. As I sat facing the sea, sometimes gray and sometimes green, most of all blue, all that living and moving and talking water carried my thoughts far away and left me empty. And when Quimet noticed I'd been quiet for a long time, he'd ask me, "Hey, how's it going?" The part I hated was when we came back zigzagging down the highway, and I could feel my soul shaking inside me and my heart was in my mouth. And Quimet said the child was getting so used to motorcycles while he was still being formed that he'd grow up to win races. "He doesn't know he's on a motorcycle, but he feels it and he'll remember it." And once we met I-don't-remember-who and I felt so embarrassed I wished the earth would open up and swallow me because he said: "She's all filled up now."

His mother gave me some undershirts Quimet had

worn when he was small and Senyora Enriqueta gave me some bandages for the belly button, which was something I still didn't understand. There were ribbons woven in and out of the lace around the collars on the shirts. They seemed made for a doll. My father said even though his name was finished if it was a boy he wanted him called Lluís and if it was a girl Margarida after his maternal great-grandmother. Quimet said that, godfather or not, he was the one who'd choose the child's name. At night when he came to bed—because he'd always stay up late making plans at the table—if I was sleeping he'd turn on the light and do everything he could to wake me up.

"Can you hear it yet?"

And when Cintet and Mateu came over he'd tell them, "It's going to be a boy as big as a house!"

I can't imagine what I must have looked like, round as a ball with my feet underneath and my head on top. One Sunday Quimet's mother showed me something very strange that looked like a dried-out root rolled into a ball. She said it was a rose of Jericho she'd been saving ever since she had Quimet and when my time came she'd put it in some water and when the rose opened, I'd open up too.

And a mania seized me for cleaning house. I'd always been very neat anyway, but now a mania seized me for cleaning. All day long I'd polish and dust and when I'd dusted everything I'd dust it all over again. I spent hours and hours polishing a faucet and if I could see a shadow when I got done, I'd start over again. I was fascinated by the way it shone. Quimet wanted me to press his pants every week. I'd never pressed pants and the first time I didn't know how to go about it. They came out with a double crease in back from the knees up, even though I'd been very careful. I slept badly and bumped into everything. When I woke up I'd spread my hands wide open in front of my eyes and look at them to see if they were still mine and if I was still me. My bones ached when I got out of bed. And Quimet started complaining furiously about his leg. Senyora Enriqueta said Quimet's sickness was called tuberculosis of the bones and he needed sulfur. But when I told Quimet he said he didn't want to explode because of Senyora Enriqueta. And when I prepared a teaspoonful of honey mixed with purified sulfur he said the honey would hurt his teeth and the whole rest of the day he talked about a dream he'd had about his teeth, that he'd been touching them one by one with the tip of his tongue and every time he touched one it came loose and was like a pebble inside his mouth. And he'd ended up with his mouth full of pebbles and he couldn't spit them out because his lips were sewn together. And whenever he had that dream he always felt like his teeth were loose afterwards and how the dream meant he was going to die. And how his teeth hurt. The grocer's wife downstairs said I should give him poppy juice to gargle, because opium puts you to sleep and the poppy juice would put the pain to sleep, but Senyora Enriqueta said maybe the poppy juice would put the pain to sleep but afterwards it would wake up again. "What Quimet needs is a good pair of dentist's tongs. Then he'll get rid of those dreams."

And while we were going through all that about his teeth and the pebbles and the death dream, I broke out in a rash that drove me crazy. At night we'd go for walks as far as a little park because I had to get some exercise. My hands were swollen, my ankles were swollen and all they needed to make me fly was to tie a string around my leg and give me a push. Hanging the clothes out to dry on the roof, surrounded by wind and blue, or sitting and sewing or walking around, I felt like they'd emptied me out of myself and filled me with something very strange. Someone I couldn't see kept blowing into my mouth and played at inflating me. Sitting on the roof, alone in the late afternoon and surrounded by railings, wind, and blueness, I'd look at my feet and while I was looking at them, without understanding what was happening, I let out my first scream.

And that first scream almost deafened me. I'd never thought my voice could carry so far and last so long. And that all the pain would come out my mouth in screams and the child down below. Quimet paced up and down in the hall praying paternosters one after the other. And once, when the midwife went out to get hot water, she told him, "Green and yellow. Believe me, I could have done without it."

When his mother saw I had a moment of rest she came over to me. "If you could see how worried Quimet is . . ." The midwife tied a towel between the bedposts and made me hold on with both hands so I could put all my strength into it. And when it was almost over one of the bedposts broke, and I heard a voice that sounded so far away I couldn't tell whose it was: "She almost suffocated it."

When I could breathe again I heard a cry and the midwife was holding a baby that looked like a little animal by his feet and it was mine. She slapped it on the back. The rose of Jericho was completely open on the night table. I passed my hand over a crocheted flower on the bedspread and tugged at one of the petals like in a dream. And they said it wasn't over, that they had to wrap the baby up. And they wouldn't let me sleep even though I couldn't keep my eyes open. . . . I couldn't even feed him. One of my breasts was small and flat like usual and the other was full of milk. Quimet said he'd thought I was going to pull some stunt on them. The boy—it was a boy—weighed almost nine pounds when he was born; a month later he weighed five. "He's melting away," Quimet said. He was melting away like a lump of sugar in a glass of water. "When he's down to a pound he'll die, just when we've finally got him."

The first time she came to see the baby, Senyora Enriqueta had already heard the story from the grocer's wife downstairs. "She says you practically strangled it." Quimet was very annoyed and paced up and down. "More work for me. I've got to make a new bedpost because the way she broke it, it can't be glued back together." The baby cried all night. As soon as it got dark he burst into tears. Quimet's mother said he was crying because he was afraid of the dark and Quimet said he couldn't tell the difference between night and day. Nothing would make him be quiet—not the pacifier or the bottle or walking around with him or yelling at him. Finally Quimet lost patience and the blood rushed to his head. He said no one could live like that and it just couldn't go on because if it lasted much longer he'd be the one who'd die.

He put the baby and the cradle in a little room next to the dining room and when we went to bed we'd shut the door. The downstairs neighbors must have heard him crying, because people started saying we were bad parents. I offered him milk and he didn't want it. I offered him water and he didn't want it. I offered him orange juice and he spat it out. When I changed him he'd cry. When I bathed him he'd cry. He was nervous. He was turning into a little monkey with legs like twigs. When he was undressed he cried louder than when he was dressed, and he wiggled his toes like they were fingers and I was afraid he'd burst. That he'd split open at the belly button. Because the swelling still hadn't gone down and you could see something had to give. The first time I got to see what he looked like, when the midwife showed me how to hold him when I gave him a bath, she told me while she was putting him in the sink:

"Before they're born they're like pears. We've all hung from this cord."

And she showed me how to take him out of the cradle holding his head because she said if I didn't hold his head his bones were so fragile I could break his neck. And she said over and over how the belly button is the most important part of the body. As important as the soft spot on your head when it still hasn't hardened. And the boy got more wrinkled every day. And the skinnier he got the more he cried. It was easy to see he was sick of living. Julieta came to see me and brought me a white kerchief with ladybugs on it. And some chocolates. She said people only think of the child and no one remembers the mother. And she said the baby was going to die, that we shouldn't worry about it any more, that a baby who wouldn't suck was as good as dead. Milk started dripping from one of my breasts. It was hard to get it out. I'd always heard people say how mother's milk is very ladylike, but I never realized how much . . . till finally, very slowly, he started to suck on the bottle. My breast got better and Quimet's mother came to get her rose of Jericho, which had closed up again, and she took it away wrapped in tissue paper.

Senyora Enriqueta grabbed the boy's neck—his name was Antoni—and shouted "A chestnut! A little chestnut!" And the boy laughed and she took him up close so he could look at the lobsters and as soon as he saw them he looked worried. And he puckered up his lips and started spitting: "Brrrr . . . Brrrr . . ." Quimet began complaining about his leg again, how it hurt even more than before because, apart from the burning, sometimes inside the bone and sometimes all around it he felt a sharp pain on his other side near the waist. "Something's pressing on the nerve," he kept saying. One day Senyora Enriqueta told me she'd always thought he was full of vim and vigor and in the best of health and I told her it hurt so much he couldn't sleep at night.

"You really believe that? When his cheeks are so rosy and his eyes sparkle like diamonds?"

Quimet's mother took care of the boy on Mondays so I could do a thorough washing. Quimet said he didn't like it one bit that his mother was taking care of the boy because he knew her and one day, while she was tying and untying bows, she'd leave the boy on the table and he'd roll off and fall on the floor like happened to him when he was less than a year old. I'd go in the afternoon to look at the dolls, holding the boy in my arms. They were still there with their round cheeks, their glass eyes set into their faces, their little noses and half-opened mouths, always laughing and delighted. And their foreheads up above, shiny near the hair from the glue they'd stuck it on with. Some of them were lying down or standing up.

Dressed in blue, in pink, with curly lace collars, with bows on their waists and tarlatan around the bottoms of their dresses to stiffen them. Their patent leather shoes gleamed in the light. Their socks were white and pulled up, their knees painted a darker flesh color than their legs. They were always there, so pretty in the shop window, waiting for people to buy them and take them away. The dolls were always there with their porcelain faces and pasteboard flesh, beside the feather dusters and mattress beaters, the chamois dustcloths: all in the store with the oilcloth.

I remember the dove and the funnel, because Quimet bought the funnel the day before the dove came. He saw the dove one day when he was about to open the dining-room balcony doors. One of its wings was broken. It was half dead and had left a trail of blood behind it. It was young. I nursed it back to health and Quimet said we should keep it, that he'd make a cage for it on the balcony so we could watch it from the dining room: a cage like a mansion, with an iron balcony, a red roof, and a door with a knocker. And how that dove would be the boy's pride and joy. We kept it for a few days with one of its legs tied to the balcony railing. Cintet came by and said we should set it free, that it probably belonged to some neighbor because if not, it wouldn't have been able to fly as far as our balcony with it wing all covered with blood. We went up on the roof and looked around, and we couldn't see a single dovecote. Cintet, with his mouth twisted, said he couldn't understand it. Mateu said the best thing was to kill it, that it was better for it to die than to live tied up like a prisoner. Then Quimet brought it in from the balcony and put it in the shed on the roof and said he'd changed his mind, that instead of building it a house he'd build a dovecote, and his apprentice's father, who raised doves, would let us have a dove on trial to see if it would mate with ours.

The apprentice came by with a dove in a basket. It wasn't till the third try that we found a mate. We named the dove we'd found Coffee, because he had a coffee-colored half moon under one wing. We named his mate Maringa. Coffee and Maringa, up in the shed on the roof, didn't have chicks. They had eggs but not chicks. Senyora Enriqueta said the male was bad and we should get rid of him. "Who knows where he came from?" she said. And she said maybe he was a carrier pigeon they'd fed strange things to so he'd get worked up and fly higher. When I told Quimet what Senyora Enriqueta had said he told me she'd be better off minding her own business, that she had enough to think about roasting chestnuts. Quimet's mother said we had no idea how much money it would end up costing us if we built a dovecote. I don't remember who it was told us we should collect nettles and hang them to dry out in bundles on the ceiling and then grind them up fine and mix them with wet bread and feed them to the doves; that it'd make them very strong and they'd lay eggs that would hatch. Senyora Enriqueta told me how she'd known an Italian lady named Flora Caravella who'd led quite a life and when she was old and mature she set up house with a few other Flora Caravellas and for amusement they had a dovecote on the roof. And she fed them nettles. And that yes, Quimet's mother was right to want to feed them nettles and when I said it wasn't Quimet's mother who'd told me about the nettles she said, "It doesn't matter. Whoever it was, they were right to say you should feed them nettles." And the wounded dove and the funnel were two things that came into our house at almost the same time, because the day before we found the dove, Quimet bought a funnel to pour wine from the carafe into the bottles. The funnel was white with a dark blue border, and he said I should be careful because if I had bad luck and it fell on the floor the edges would get chipped.

We built the dovecote. The day Quimet had chosen to start work it rained cats and dogs. And he set up his carpenter's shop in the dining room. They nailed the frame together and prepared everything in the dining room. They carried the door, finished from top to bottom with a balcony and everything, from the dining room to the roof. Cintet came over to help us and the first Sunday when the weather was nice we all went up to the roof to watch Mateu, who was in the shed building a window with a wide sill so the doves could rest for a moment and think about where they wanted to land before they flew down to the ground. He took everything I had out of the shed: my clothes basket, my chairs, my hamper for dirty clothes, my basket full of clothesline.

"We're evicting Colometa."

They promised me that later on they'd build another shed where I could keep my things, but for the moment I had to bring everything down to the apartment and if I wanted to sit on the roof for a while I had to bring up a chair. They said the dovecote had to be painted before they could let the doves loose in it. One wanted to paint it green, another blue, and another chocolate-color. They decided to paint it blue, and I was the painter. Because once the dovecote was finished Quimet always had to work on Sundays and he said if we waited too long to paint it the rain would ruin the wood. So I painted while Antoni slept or lay on the roof and cried. Three coats. And the day the paint was dry we all went up to the roof and we let the doves loose inside the dovecote. First the white one came out of his cage, with red eyes and red feet with black claws. Then came the black one, with black feet and gray eyes with thin yellow rings around them. Both of them spent quite a while looking around before they flew out. They bobbed their heads up and down a few times. It seemed like they were about to go out, but then they thought it over again. And finally, beating their wings, they flew out. One landed beside the water dish, the other beside the food tray. And she shook her head and neck like a lady in mourning so the feathers sort of ruffled up, and he went over to her and spread his tail and round and round they went, billing and cooing. And Quimet was the first one to speak because we were all keeping quiet, and he said the doves were happy.

He said when they'd learned to go in and out the window and only the window he'd open the door and then they'd be able to go out both ways, but if he opened the door before they were used to going out the window they'd only go out the door. Then he put in roosts for them because up to then we'd been using roosts the apprentice's father had lent us. When everything was ready, Quimet asked if there was any blue paint left and I said yes and he had me paint the balcony railing. A week later he brought home two very strange doves with a kind of cowl that made them look neckless and he said they were called nuns. And he named them Monk and Nun. They immediately started quarreling with the first pair, who didn't want newcomers and who were masters of the dovecote, but little by little the nuns, by keeping out of the way and enduring a little hunger and an occasional swat with a wing and keeping to the corners, finally managed to get the older ones used to them and ended up being the masters themselves. Whatever they wanted they got, and if they didn't get it they'd chase the others with their cowls spread open. And two weeks later Quimet came back with another pair of turkeytail doves, very vain: all the time with their chests stuck out and their tails in the air, and then the old ones started laying eggs and everything went well.

The smells of meat and fish and flowers and vegetables all mixed together and even if I hadn't had eyes I'd have realized I was getting near the market square. I'd come out of my street, across the Carrer Gran with yellow streetcars going up and down ringing their bells and with the drivers and conductors wearing striped uniforms with stripes so thin that everything looked gray. The sunlight came up the Passeig de Gràcia and wham!—between the rows of buildings it fell on the sidewalk, the people, the stone slabs under the balconies. The street sweepers were sweeping with big brooms made of heather twigs, looking as though they were thinking of something far away. They were sweeping the gutters.

I made my way into the smell of the market till I was in the middle of all that shoving—in a thick river of women and baskets. My shellfish seller, with blue half-sleeves and an apron with a bib, was dishing out pound after pound of mussels and scallops that she'd washed with fresh water but which still had the smell of the sea inside their shells and it spread through the air. The sweet smell of death came from the rows of offal sellers. They made use of all the animals' guts, selling them spread out on cabbage leaves: kids' feet, kids' heads with glazed eyes, hearts cut in half with an empty tube in the middle clogged with a bit of blood that had gotten stuck there: a drop of black blood. Livers soaked through with blood and wet tripe and boiled heads hanging from hooks and all the offal sellers had white, waxy faces from spending so much time near such tasteless foods, from blowing so much into pink lungs with their backs turned to the customers as if it was a sin. My fish seller, laughing through her gold teeth, was weighing some fresh cod, and the light bulb hanging above her shone, so tiny you almost couldn't see it, from every fish scale. The mullet, the flying fish, the haddock, the groupers with their big heads, looking like they'd just been painted with their spines pressing against their backs like the thorns on a big flower—all the fish came from those waves that left me empty when I sat and watched them. They came out with their tails flapping and their eyes bulging. My vegetable seller had saved some brussels sprouts for me—an old thin woman always dressed in black, with two sons who took care of her gardens.

And everything went along like this, with little headaches, till the Republic came and Quimet got all excited and went marching through the streets shouting and waving a flag. I never could figure out where he got it from. I still remember that cool air, an air that—every time I think of it—I've never smelled again. Never. Mixed with the smell of new leaves and the smell of flower buds; an air that couldn't last, and the air that came afterwards was never like the air on that day—a day that made a notch in my life, because it was with that April and those flower-buds that my little headaches started turning into big headaches.

"They had to pack their suitcases, grab them, and make a quick getaway to France!" said Cintet, and he said the king slept with three different showgirls every night and the queen had to wear a disguise just to go out in the street. And Quimet said everything still wasn't known.

Cintet and Mateu came over a lot and Mateu was more in love with Griselda every day and he'd say, "When I'm with Griselda my heart pounds so I'm afraid it'll burst." And Quimet and Cintet said they thought he was sick in the head because love was weakening his brain and he kept right on talking about his Griselda and it was true that he couldn't talk about anything else and he was becoming like an idiot even though I was very fond of him. And he said the day he'd gotten married he'd been the one who couldn't stand on his feet he was so carried away, because he said men are more sensitive than women, and how he'd almost fainted when they were about to be alone together. And Quimet, rocking a little in his chair, laughed through his nose and he and Cintet told Mateu he should go in for some sport because if his body was tired his brain wouldn't work so hard, and if he kept thinking about the same thing all day long he'd end up in a shirt with long sleeves tied behind his back with a sailor's knot. And they talked about which sport would suit him best and he said being a foreman at a building site and running around keeping an eye on the work was already enough exercise and if in addition they wanted to tire him out playing soccer, for example, or going swimming at the Astillero, he'd end up not being able to satisfy his Griselda and she'd look for another man who'd pay more attention to her.

They argued a lot about all this, but when Mateu brought Griselda they couldn't talk freely or give him advice. So they'd wind up talking about the Republic or about the doves and their chicks. Because Quimet, as soon as he saw the conversation dying down, would take them up to the roof and tell them how the doves lived and which ones were mates. He told them how some stole the others' mates and others always stayed with the same mate and how the chicks would grow up healthy because he made them drink water with sulfur in it. And they spent hours discussing whether Patxulí was preparing a roost for Tigrada and how the first dove Coffee, the one with little red eyes and black claws who came to our balcony bleeding, had had his first children all covered with dark half moons and with gray feet. Quimet said doves were like people. The only difference was that doves laid eggs and could fly and went around wearing feathers but as far as having children and trying to keep them fed was concerned they were just the same as the rest of us. Mateu said he didn't care for animals and that he could never eat pigeons he'd raised at his house because he felt like killing a pigeon who'd been born at his house would be like killing someone in the family. And Quimet poked him in the stomach and said, "Wait till you're good and hungry. . . ."

It was Cintet's doing that the doves came out of the dovecote and we let them fly around, because he said doves had to fly, that they weren't made to live behind bars but up in the blue sky. And they opened the door wide and Quimet stood there with his hands on his head looking like he'd been turned to stone. "We'll never see them again."

The doves, very distrustfully, slowly came out of the dovecote, one after another, scared to death that it was some kind of trick. Some of them flew onto the railing and looked around before taking off. The thing was they weren't used to being free and they waited a while before flying. Only three or four of them took off right away. But then some others joined them till there were nine. Because the others were nesting. And when Quimet saw the doves flying above our roof and only above our roof, his face stopped looking so yellow and he said everything was okay. When the doves got sick of flying they started to come down, first one and then another. They went back in the dovecote like old ladies going to mass, taking little steps and jerking their heads like wind-up toys. From then on I couldn't hang clothes on the roof because the doves would get them dirty. I had to hang them on the balcony. And be grateful for that.

Quimet said the boy needed fresh air and the open road. Enough hanging around the roof and the balcony and grandma's little garden. He built a wooden box like a cradle and attached it to the motorcycle. He picked up the boy like a bundle—he was less than a year old—and strapped him into the box and took his bottle along. Whenever I saw them go off I always felt like I'd never see them again. Senyora Enriqueta said Quimet didn't show his feelings much but he was crazy about the boy. That she'd never seen anything like it. And as soon as they left I'd go and open the balcony doors above the street so I'd be able to hear the motorcycle putt-putting when they came back. Quimet would take the boy out of his box—he was almost always asleep—and run up the stairs four at a time and give him to me: "Here. Take him, full of health and fresh air. He'll sleep for a week straight."

A year and a half later, exactly a year and a half after I had the boy, surprise! It happened again. I had a very rough pregnancy, always sick as a dog. And sometimes Quimet would run his finger under my eyes and say, "Violets . . . violets . . . it's going to be a girl." And I was worried sick when I saw them go off on the motorcycle and Senyora Enriqueta told me I had to control myself because if I worried too much, the baby inside would turn over and they'd have to pull it out with tongs. And Quimet started saying he wondered if I'd break the bedpost, that if I broke it this time he'd replace it with one that had an iron bar inside. And he'd say no one knew how I'd kept him dancing and how much dancing he'd still have to do to pay for that first dance in the Plaça del Diamant. Violets . . . "Roses are red, violets are blue, Colometa's little nose in between the two." Violets . . . violets . . .

It was a girl. They named her Rita. I barely found out about it because the blood poured out of me like a river and they couldn't stop it. Antoni got jealous of the girl and we had to keep a close watch on him. One day I found he'd climbed up on a stool next to the cradle. He was stuffing his toy top down the girl's throat and when I got there she was already half dead, her face white as a coconut or one of those Chinese dolls. It was the first time I hit Antoni and three hours later he was still crying and the girl too, both of them covered with snot and misery. And while I was hitting Antoni, as little as he was, tinier than a cork, he was kicking my leg as hard as he could and ended up falling on his ass. I'd never seen anyone as angry as he got when I hit him. And when Cintet and Mateu and Griselda and their girl came to visit, if one of them said Rita was cute, the boy would go over to the cradle, climb in it as best he could, and start hitting her and pulling her hair. "Between him and the doves, that's all she needs," Griselda would say, holding her little girl on her lap, who was so pretty and who didn't know how to laugh. Griselda was indescribable: white, with a few freckles at the top of each cheek. And calm eyes that were green like mint. Slender at the waist. Pure silk. Wearing a cherry-colored dress in summer. A doll. She didn't talk much. Mateu would stare at her and while he was staring he'd melt away. . . . "We've been married so many years . . . and I'm still not used to it. . . ." And Quimet would say, "Violets. Look what violets she's got. . . . Colometa, *violeta*." Because after I had the girl, the same as before I had her, there were blue circles under my eyes.

To make Antoni forget about being jealous of Rita, Quimet bought him a nickel-plated revolver with a trigger, "click, click," and a wooden nightstick. "To scare grandma," he said. "When grandma comes, a whack on the head and bang!" Quimet was mad at his mother because she'd taught the boy to say he didn't want to go on the motorcycle because it made him sick. And he said his mother was trying to turn the boy into a girl, that it was an old mania of hers and we'd see where it would end up. And the boy learned how to act lame because he heard Quimet complaining about his leg. He didn't talk about it for a while, but when I had Rita there we were again: "Last night it burned like boiling water. Didn't you hear me groaning?" And the boy imitated him. The days when he wasn't hungry he'd tell me his leg hurt. He'd throw his soup bowl up in the air and sit on his throne as stiff as a judge and bang his fork if I didn't hurry up and bring him the little pieces of liver which were what he ate most. When he wasn't hungry he'd throw them across the room. And when Senyora Enriqueta or Quimet's mother came to see me he'd plant himself in front of them with his gun and shoot them dead. One day when Senyora Enriqueta pretended to die he got so excited that he kept on killing her over and over and we had to lock him out on the balcony so we could talk.

And then that thing started. At times Quimet would feel queasy. And he'd say, "I don't feel right," and he didn't talk about his leg, only about that awful feeling he got a little while after he'd eaten, even though he had a good appetite. As long as he was sitting at the table everything was all right, but ten minutes after he finished he'd start feeling upset. There was a little less work coming into his shop and I thought maybe he was saying he didn't feel good to avoid saying he was worried because he was getting less work. One morning when I was stripping the bed I found a bit of something like tape or like a piece of intestine with wavy edges on Quimet's side of the bed. I wrapped it up in a piece of writing paper and when Quimet came home I showed it to him and he said he'd take it to the drugstore and show it to them and he said if it was intestine he was done for.

That afternoon I couldn't hold out any longer and I took

the children and went to the shop. Quimet got mad and asked me what I was doing there and I said we just happened to be passing by but he got the idea and sent the apprentice out to buy some chocolate for the children. As soon as the apprentice shut the door behind him he said, "I don't want him to hear about it because five minutes later even the stones would know." I asked him what they'd said at the drugstore and he said they'd told him he had a tapeworm the size of a house, one of the biggest they'd ever seen. And that they'd given him something to kill it. And he said, "When the kid comes back with the chocolate, beat it. We'll talk about it tonight." The apprentice came back with the chocolate, Quimet gave some to the boy and just a little to the girl so she could lick it and we went home. He came home that night and said, "Hurry up with supper. They told me at the drugstore that if I don't eat a lot the worm will start eating me." And when he'd eaten he felt so sick I could hardly bear it and he said Sunday he'd take the medicine and pray the worm came out whole because if it didn't come out whole, from head to tail, it'd grow back again two feet longer. I asked him if they'd told him how long the worms were and he said they came in all sizes, depending on what kind and how old they were, but usually their necks alone were ten feet long.

Cintet and Mateu came to see Quimet take the medicine and he told them to go away because he had to be by himself. A couple of hours later he was staggering up and down the hall without even knowing where he was, swaying from side to side, and he said, "It's worse than being on a boat." And he growled that if he threw up the medicine all his trouble would be for nothing, and that the worm had declared war on him to make him throw it up. It wasn't until the children were sleeping like angels and I couldn't keep my eyes open and was half dead from tiredness that he vomited up the worm. We'd never seen one. It was the color of spaghetti made without eggs, and we kept it in alcohol in a jam jar. Cintet and Quimet arranged it so its neck was at the top, all twisted. The neck was as thin as a thread, with the head on top as small as a pinhead or even smaller. We kept it on top of a wardrobe and we spent more than a week talking about the tapeworm. And Quimet said now we were even because I'd had the kids and he'd had a worm fifteen yards long. One afternoon the grocer's wife came up to see it and said her grandfather used to have one too and at night when he was snoring he'd cough and choke because the worm would stick its head out his mouth. Later we went up on the roof to look at the doves. She liked them a lot and went away happy. When I got to the apartment door I could already hear the girl crying and I found her terrified in her cradle, waving her arms furiously, all covered with the worm, and when I got the worm off her and went to spank the boy he ran right in front of my nose laughing and dragging a piece of the worm behind him like it was a paper chain.

I couldn't describe how angry Quimet was. He wanted to give the boy a beating and I told him to forget it because it was our fault for not keeping the jar with the worm higher up. That ever since the day he'd stuck that top down Rita's throat we'd known how much trouble he could get into with the stool. And Cintet told him not to get worked up, that maybe he'd have another worm soon that he could put in a jar because it was already growing inside him. But it wasn't true.

And business got very slow for Quimet. He said new jobs weren't coming in but that everything would be all right in the end, that people had changed and weren't thinking about having furniture restored or new stuff made. That the rich were mad at the Republic. And my children—I don't know, because everyone knows how mothers exaggerate, but they were as pretty as two flowers. They wouldn't have won any first prizes, but they were like two flowers. With eyes . . . with eyes that gazed at you and when you saw them gazing at you with those eyes . . . I don't know how Quimet could bring himself to scold the boy so often. I scolded him once in a while, but only when he'd done something really naughty. Otherwise I'd let him get away with anything. The house wasn't like before; it wasn't like when we'd gotten married. At times—you could even say all the time—it looked like a bazaar. Not to mention when we built the dovecote, which was total madness, everything covered with sawdust and wood shavings and twisted tacks. . . . And he couldn't get work and we all had to go hungry and I hardly saw Quimet because I don't know what kind of mischief he and Cintet were up to. And I couldn't stay at home twiddling my thumbs, so one day I decided to look for a part-time job in the mornings. I'd lock the kids in the dining room and explain everything to the boy because if I spoke to him like an adult he'd listen to me and a morning goes by quickly.

When I needed a rest I'd go see Senyora Enriqueta. I

showed up alone and trembling—not at Senyora Enriqueta's house but at the house of some people Senyora Enriqueta had told me to go see because they needed someone to help out in the mornings. I rang the bell. I waited. I rang the bell again. I waited some more. And when I'd started thinking I was ringing the bell at an empty house, I heard a voice just as a truck went by and with the racket I couldn't hear what the voice was saying. I was standing at an iron door with frosted glass and on the other side of the frosted glass, which had little bubbles in it for decoration, I saw a sheet of paper stuck on with tape and the paper said: "Ring at the garden gate." I rang the bell again and I heard the voice again, coming from a window next to the door: a window just above the ground, right under the balcony. The balcony had an iron grille on it from top to bottom. The window above the ground had a grille too, and in addition there was a metal screen like chicken wire but better than chicken wire. The voice said: "Go around the corner!"

For a moment I was confused and stood there thinking and then I looked through the glass bubbles at the sheet of paper on the other side and finally I understood a little and stuck my head around the corner, because the house was on a corner. About fifty yards away I saw a little gate to the garden. It was half open and a gentleman was standing there wearing a long smock and he waved to me to come over. And that gentleman in the smock was tall, with very dark eyes. He looked like a good person. He asked me if I was the woman who was looking for work in the morning. I said yes. To get into the garden I had to go down four brick steps, a little worn away at the edges, that went under a trellis covered with jasmine—the kind with little flowers, the kind that drowns you in its smell as soon as the sun goes down. I saw a fountain coming out of the wall on my left at the end of the garden, and a round fountain in the middle. The gentleman in the smock and I went through the garden and into the house, which from behind was just two floors, and in front it was just the basement and the first floor. The garden was long and narrow. It had two mandarin orange trees, an apricot tree, and a lemon tree with its trunk and the bottoms of the leaves covered with some kind of disease that made little bubbles that were like spiderwebs inside where the insects lived. There was a cherry tree next to the lemon tree inside the fountain, and a tall mimosa without many leaves. It had the same disease as the lemon tree. I noticed all this later on, of course.

To get into the ground floor you had to go through a cement courtyard with a hole in the middle so the rainwater could drain away. The cement was full of cracks. The cracks had little piles of dirt and sand on them, and ants would come out of them like soldiers. It was the ants that made the little piles of sand. On the courtyard wall facing the neighbors there were four leather wine jugs with camellias growing in them, also a little diseased. On the other side there was a staircase to the second floor. Under this staircase there were some washbasins and a well with a pulley. After the courtyard you came to a covered porch and the roof of this porch was the floor of the open porch on the second floor. There were two balconies leading onto the bottom porch: one from the dining room and one from the kitchen. I don't know if I'm explaining it clearly. And I and the gentleman in the smock, who was the son-in-law of the owners and was in charge of the house, went into the dining room.

He had me sit down in a chair by the wall. Above my

head there was a window that touched the dining-room ceiling, which made a half arch. But the bottom of this window was level with the sidewalk where I'd come in the garden gate. As soon as I sat down a lady with white hair came in. She was the gentleman in the smock's mother-in-law. She sat down opposite me, but the table was between us, with a vase of flowers that made it hard to see her. The man in the smock remained standing. A thin, yellowish-looking little boy came out from under a wicker armchair with cretonne cushions and stood beside the lady, who was his grandma, and looked at us one after the other. I spoke with the man in the smock. He told me there were four in the family: the two in-laws and the two young people who were himself and his wife—that is, his in-laws' daughter—and that he and his wife lived with the in-laws, "My wife's parents, I mean." While the gentleman in the smock talked he kept touching his Adam's apple and he said, "Some families only need a cleaning woman one day out of five." And how those families were bad for someone who wanted a steady wage because a woman who worked there never knew what sickness she'd die from. So the wage was three *rals* an hour, but since the work was steady and all year round and they paid on time and I'd never have to ask twice for what I earned and they'd pay me for every day when I finished if I wanted them to, instead of three *pessetes* for four hours they'd pay me ten *rals*. Because it was as if instead of selling it retail—since I was selling them my work—I was selling it wholesale and everyone knows when you sell wholesale there's a discount. And he said everyone knew he paid promptly, more promptly than the promptest man in the world, not like some unfortunates who when the end of the month comes they already owe for the next one.

He sort of overwhelmed me and we settled on ten *rals* and then the lady, who'd been quiet all that time, said she'd show me the house.

The kitchen was next to the dining room and also led to the porch and there was a big chimney with a hood that came down over the stove like in an old-fashioned kitchen, even though they didn't use it since they cooked with gas. You could see it was full of soot because when it was about to rain pieces of soot would fall on the burners. There was a glass door at the end of the dining room which led to a hallway and there was a very big, heavy wardrobe in the hallway and when the house was quiet you could hear the termites serenading. That wardrobe was the termites' dining room. Sometimes I even heard them first thing in the morning and I told the lady about it.

"The sooner they polish it off the better."

So we went down that hallway with the wardrobe and into a living room with an alcove that they'd modernized; they'd ripped out the glass that separated the two rooms and the only thing left was the mark on the ceiling. There was another wardrobe made of black mahogany in this living room, with a mirror covered with specks. Right under the window that touched the ceiling, like the window in the dining room, there was a dressing table with a mirror that also had a lot of specks on it and next to it there was a new sink with shiny faucets. In the alcove there were shelves up to the ceiling all around, all full of books and on the far side was a bookcase with wooden doors on the bottom and glass on top and one of the panes was shattered and the lady told me her daughter had shattered it, the mother of the yellowish boy who kept following us the whole time, and how she'd shattered it with an airgun the boy had gotten for Christmas: an airgun with rubber darts. You could see she must have been a knucklehead because she'd aimed at the light bulb that hung from a wire above the table but her aim was so bad that instead of hitting the bulb she'd shattered a pane in the bookcase doors.

"And that's how it happened," the lady said.

And in the middle of the alcove there was a table covered by a sheet that had been burned with an iron, where the white-haired lady's husband (who was the only one in the house who went to work and I barely caught sight of him the whole time I was there) would read at night. They ironed clothes on that table. The wall against the bathroom and the wall with the window were covered with mildew because it was the basement and when it rained water would seep in and run down the walls. Next to this room, at the end of the hallway where the wardrobe was with the termites, the lady opened a little door: the bath. They called it Nero's Bath. It was squared at the corners and was made of very old glazed tiles, badly fitted together and a lot of them chipped. The lady told me they only used it during the hottest part of summer and then just to shower because they'd have had to empty the sea to fill up that bathtub. And above the bathtub you could see a dull light coming through a piece of glass that was a trapdoor leading to the entrance up above where the grille was with the sign taped to it, and sometimes they'd lift the glass to air out the bathroom and they'd prop it up with a bamboo stick. And I asked what would happen if the boy lifted the glass and looked in while one of the grownups was bathing. And the lady said, "Be quiet." And the ceiling and the bit of wall above the glazed tiles, since they weren't covered by tiles, were like the living room and the alcove—full of mildew that sparkled like glass when you looked at it close up. But she said the worst part was that when they emptied the tub it took a long time for all the water to drain out because the sewer in the street was a little higher up than the bathtub and how sometimes, if the sewer wouldn't suck out the water, they had to empty it with ladles and mops.

Then we went up a winding staircase to the first floor, which was really the second floor. Halfway up the stairs there was a window that looked out on the street where the garden gate was and when they were all upstairs and people rang at the garden gate they'd yell through the window to come in the door with the sign on it. As you climbed the staircase you could see the top of the wardrobe with the termites, all covered with dust. And we came out in the front hall with the boy behind us. We were standing in front of a dark carved wooden chest and an umbrella stand shaped like an upside-down umbrella, with old clothes and hats hanging from the spokes. If Quimet could have seen that chest he'd have fallen in love with it immediately. I told the lady and she ran her finger along the carvings on top and said, "You know what it represents?"

"No, senyora."

There were a boy and a girl right in the middle of the top, just their heads with very big noses and lips like Negroes, looking at each other. And she said, "It represents the eternal question: love." And the boy laughed.

We went into a room that had a balcony overlooking the street right above the window where the woman had shouted to me to ring at the garden gate. It was another modernized living room with an alcove. There was a black piano and two small pink velvet-covered armchairs and a piece of furniture with very strange legs on it, as high as a horse's legs, and the lady told me she'd personally had her restorer make them to hold up that piece of furniture, which was a chest with little drawers all inlaid with mother-of-pearl, and she said they were faun's legs. The bed in the alcove was old, made of some kind of gold-plated metal with just one column on each side at the foot. At the head there was a wooden Christ in a little niche with his hands tied together and a sour look on his face, wearing a red and gold tunic. The lady said it was the young people's room but that the old people—she and her husband, that is—slept there because her daughter couldn't fall asleep with all the cars going up and down the street and she preferred to sleep in the back bedroom with the calm of the garden. There was a little door next to the bed with the Christ. It led to a little windowless bedroom where there was a bed with a blue mosquito net over it. Nothing else would have fit there. It was where the boy who kept following us slept.

Then we went into the main living room. The first thing I saw was a chest all gilded from top to bottom, gold and blue with colored shields all around the bottom and a Saint Eulalia on top sticking up in the air and holding a golden lily in one hand, and a dragon nearby with his tail twisted on top of a treeless mountain and his mouth wide open and three tongues of fire like three flames. "It's a Gothic hope chest," the lady said. The chest was in front of the balcony that was right above the dining-room window that touched the ceiling. And there was another balcony on the right as you came out of the boy's bedroom and it led to the open porch. She couldn't show me the young people's bedroom—which was really the old people's bedroom—because her daughter was resting. And she and the boy started walking on tiptoe and so did I.

We went out onto the open porch on the first floor which was really the second floor, and went down the stairs above the well and the fountain into the cement courtyard, which was always full of skittles because the boy liked to play there. The lady explained that her daughter needed rest because she was sick and she told me about her daughter's illness, that she'd gotten it when she tried to move the leather jugs with the camellias. The next day she'd passed blood. The doctor told them the only way he could be sure what was wrong with her would be to take out one of her kidneys. And the doctor, who wasn't their regular one because he was on vacation, had told them this when they were standing on the marble stairs at the main entrance, next to the glass trapdoor above that bathtub with glazed tiles.

Before I left she showed me how to open the garden gate from the street. The gate had a sheet of iron along the bottom and iron bars at the top but since some kids had kept throwing garbage in the garden—one time they even threw in a dead rabbit—her son-in-law, the gentleman in the smock, that is, boarded it up on the inside. The bars and the lock were on the outside and all you could see from the garden side was the keyhole. They only locked it at night, and to open it from the street during the day you had to tug on the lock and stick your hand through the crack and unhook the chain that was attached to a hook on thc wall. It was very simple, but you had to know how to do it. And if I've spent so much time talking about the house it's because it's still a puzzle to me with those people's voices that when they called me I never knew where they were coming from.

Quimet said if I wanted to get a job that was my business and for his part he'd try to make some money raising doves. And how we could get rich selling doves. I went to Senyora Enriqueta's house to tell her about the interview I'd had with my bosses. And while I was on my way the streets, which were the same size as ever, seemed narrower to me. As soon as we got there the boy climbed up on a chair so he could see the lobsters. Senyora Enriqueta told me she'd look after the kids, that she'd take them to the corner in front of the Smart Cinema and make them sit in a little chair next to her. Antoni climbed down off the chair he'd been standing on and since he'd understood everything he said he wanted to stay at home. I told Senyora Enriqueta she could get the boy to stay put because he'd obey when he felt like it but that Rita, poor thing, was too tiny to spend all morning sitting in the street. With the buzz of conversation Rita had fallen asleep in my lap and the boy had gotten up on the chair again, glued to the lobsters. It was drizzling outside. I don't know why, but whenever I went to see Senyora Enriqueta it was a miracle if it didn't rain. The drops slid along the clotheslines till some of them, the most swollen ones, stretched till they looked like tears and then fell to the ground.

The day I started working in that basement house, what a joke! The water stopped when I'd half finished washing the dishes. The lady told the gentleman in the smock and they both came down to the kitchen, looking very dignified. He turned on the faucet and when he saw that not a drop of water came out he said he'd go up on the roof and see what was up, because they had the water tank half open so they could see right away what the water level was and leaves would sometimes get stuck in the hole where the water flowed out. The lady told me to dust the dining room while I was waiting and I thought that's where I'd locked my own children because Quimet had agreed that Senyora Enriqueta wouldn't be able to keep an eye on them, that her mind would wander and maybe the boy would get away from her and run out in the street and get run over. And while I was dusting with a cloth, because the lady said feather dusters just scattered the dust around and when you turned your back it went back where you'd just dusted, the daughter came down and said hello to me and I thought she looked very healthy.

The lady told me to draw a bucket of water from the well to wash the window up against the ceiling. Since it was at street level and carts and trucks went by all day it was always covered with dust or mud when it rained. A sprinkle here and a sprinkle there and she certainly kept me hopping. The gentleman in the smock came down and from the landing of the winding staircase where you came out in the front hall he said there wasn't enough water, that the pipe leading out of the tank wasn't clogged but no water was coming in because it was probably clogged at the entrance from the street. Then the lady told me to bring up a few more buckets of water from the well so I could finish washing the dishes even though she was scared of that water because she always thought sometime or other they'd thrown someone in to drown. But that there was a danger that the man from the company wouldn't come for two or three days and we certainly couldn't be all that time without water.

And with a few more buckets of water I was able to finish the dishes while the lady dried them. The daughter had disappeared. And I went to make the beds. I got to them by climbing the garden staircase above the fountain. The boy was playing next to the fountain in the middle of the courtyard. He thought no one was watching him and he threw a handful of sand inside and then he noticed me. He turned white, with his eyes very still, as if he was made of stone. While I was making the bed in the front bedroom—the one with the balcony that looked out above the window the voice had come from the first day telling me to ring at the garden—the lady called me from the bathroom and her voice came through the glass trapdoor. She told me to open the little closet with the gas and inside I'd find a folded card and that I should fold it over the sign telling people to ring at the garden gate because if they made the man from the water company go out of his way maybe he'd get mad at them for having him make such a long detour. That the card would stand up because of the way it was folded with a pleat at the top and they'd made it specially so they wouldn't have to take the sign off and put it back again each time.

I stuck the white card between the glass and the sign, and it stood up very well because of the fold. And the lady came up to see if I'd understood and she showed me how I could take the glass out from between the bars by lifting some latches that held it in place and how it was very easy to wash and how sometimes the latches would get stuck because they were so dirty and you had to hit them with a hammer to get them off. And how it was very practical to be able to lift the glass out of the bars because otherwise it would have been a real nuisance to wash the glass sticking your fingers between the bars. And she told me the grille had been made by an ironworker from Sants, even though their usual ironworker lived in Sant Gervasi. But her son-in-law had managed to trick the ironworker from Sants by telling him he was in charge of building a bunch of houses and needed fifty grilles and how the first one would be like a sample. Which he couldn't have said to the ironworker from Sant Gervasi, because he knew he lived off his investments. So they got the sample grille almost for free and the Sants ironworker was still sitting there waiting for the big order.

When the gentleman came back I didn't hear him come in because he must have come in the garden gate. They paid me at one o'clock and I went running through the streets, and when I was crossing the Carrer Gran I almost got run over by a streetcar and I don't know what angel saved my life. The children hadn't done anything naughty. Rita was asleep on the floor. And as soon as the boy saw me he started whining.

The man from the water company came the next day at ten in the morning and I went to let him in. The gentleman came up right away, looking very sad, and he said, "We haven't had any water since yesterday. We couldn't bathe the children and we had a very rough night."

And the man from the company, who was fat and had a mustache, raised his head from unscrewing a faucet underneath the trapdoor and laughed. The two of them went up to the roof to measure the water level and when they came down the gentleman gave the man a tip and the man put the trapdoor back on and left. I went down the winding staircase and the gentleman, who'd gone down the garden stairs, asked me to get an empty quart bottle and told me to come up with him to the roof to measure the water level because the man from the water company had measured it any which way and he had a notion that he was a very good fellow and had left twice the normal amount. We got to the roof, I held the bottle and he looked at his watch; a woman on the roof next door said hello to him and he started talking with her. She was a tenant in the house next door, which also belonged to them even though it wasn't so nicely furnished as theirs was. I called him when the bottle was full and he hurried over with his smock fluttering behind him. He looked at his watch and said they'd never had so much water and that before it took six minutes for the bottle to fill up and this time it had only taken three and a half. That night before I went to sleep I told Quimet about the ironworker from Sants and he said, "The richer they are, the weirder."

By the third day I'd already started going in without knocking, just pulling the lock and unhooking the chain. I found the lady and her son-in-law sitting in the wicker chairs underneath the balcony. I noticed right away that the gentleman in the smock had a black eye. I went in the kitchen to wash the dishes and found them all piled up dirty from the day before, and the lady came down to keep me company.

She told me they were having some problems. And she asked if I'd seen her son-in-law's black eye and I told her I'd noticed it right away. She said they had a tenant in a shed that he used as a workshop to make toy horses and that her son-in-law had found out he made a very good living off his toy horses and wanted to raise the rent. He'd gone over at lunchtime and found the tenant just sitting down to eat, because it seems they ate and lived in the same shed where they worked and they had a table and a bed in one corner. Her son-in-law went up to him and gave him a bill for the new rent and the tenant said he couldn't do that and the son-in-law said yes he could and the tenant said no he couldn't till the tenant got very mad and picked up a big lamb bone on his plate and threw it at the son-in-law and it was just his bad luck that it hit him right in the eye. And the lady said, "When you came in we were just talking about going to see our lawyer." And at that moment the bell rang and the lady asked me if I'd please go and see who it was because she still hadn't washed her face. I asked her which bell it was because I couldn't figure out where the ringing was coming from; and the lady told me the bell I'd heard was the garden bell that rang on the porch, while the main doorbell rang in the front hall at the top of the staircase. She said, "If it's someone answering our ad tell them we only rent to people without children and the house has three terraces. If they say fine, call me and we'll have them come in and my son-in-law can give them the rest of the details and conditions. Don't push the door open; you know it opens outwards and they might get hurt."

I went to open the door and I found a very well-dressed old gentleman and lady who looked very clean. They said they'd left their car in front of the main entrance and had gotten tired of pressing the bell that didn't ring till by chance they saw the sign and rang at the garden.

"We've come about the ad for the house, you see."

And the gentleman gave me a piece of newspaper he'd cut out very carefully and told me to read it. I tried to read it but I couldn't understand a word because there was a letter and then a period. Another letter and then a period. Two letters and a period. And the address. And more letters and periods without any whole words. I didn't understand a thing. I gave him back the paper and told him the landlord didn't want children. The gentleman said the house was for his son who had three children and that, as was perfectly natural, if he wanted to rent a house it was precisely because he had children, and then he said, half angry and half joking, "What's my son supposed to do with his children? Give them to King Herod?"

And they left without even saying good-by. The lady was waiting for me by the fountain, which had a little boy in the middle made out of stone, wearing a faded blue and green straw hat and holding a bunch of flowers. The water came of the middle of a daisy. The gentleman was standing on the porch watching us and brushing his teeth with a towel wrapped around his neck because the cork was worn out in the bathroom faucet and they'd tied it with a piece of string so the water wouldn't keep gushing out. And he was washing up in the kitchen. I told the lady it was a married couple, a gentleman and a lady, and how they hadn't liked it at all when they heard about the children. I told her they'd gotten tired of pressing the upstairs bell and how it didn't ring. The lady said sometimes people were tiresome and even after reading the sign they'd still ring and then they'd shut off the current and people could ring to their hearts' content.

While we were waiting for the gentleman to finish brushing his teeth we looked at the goldfish in the fountain. His name was Balthasar because they'd given him to the boy on the Three Kings' day and it was named after one of them. I asked her why they didn't want children in the house and she said it was because children broke everything and her son-in-law didn't want them. We went towards the house and just when I was walking across the cement courtyard, the garden bell! The advertisement again. I ran to open the door and it was a young man, and the first thing he said was that the house was like a centipede, that they'd given him one address and then made him walk three miles to get in.

My bosses always had houses for rent and I always had to go and explain the whole story and sometimes before they rented a house, since they asked for so many things, they'd spend three or four months looking for a tenant.

I decided to leave the children with Senyora Enriqueta, because being cooped up in the dining room wasn't any kind of life. She was happy to have them and took a scarf and tied the girl to a little chair. And she said she should have had them right from the first day I began working. I told her not to give them peanuts because they'd eat themselves sick and I made them promise not to ask for any because it'd spoil their appetite for lunch. It didn't last long. The boy got restless and said he wanted to go home. That he didn't like being in the street. That I should let him stay in the apartment and that he wanted to be in the apartment. So I let them stay there because it was true that during the time I'd left them alone nothing had happened.

Till one day when I came in I heard a roar of wings and the boy was standing on the balcony with his back to the street and his arm around Rita, and they were very still. But since as soon as I got home I had to hurry and make lunch for everyone I didn't pay much attention. They'd gotten in the habit of playing with birdseed. Each one had a little box full of birdseed and they made designs on the floor with it: paths and flowers and stars.

By now we had ten pairs of doves and one day at lunchtime when Quimet was coming back from seeing a gentleman who lived near where I worked, he came to pick me up and I introduced him to the lady. I went off with Quimet and on the way home I did an errand for the lady and left a list at the grocery store. When I came out Quimet, who'd stayed outside, asked if I'd noticed that the birdseed in that grocery store was the best he'd ever seen, that he'd noticed it when we'd just gotten engaged, and he had me go back inside and buy ten pounds of birdseed. The grocer weighed it for me himself. He looked like Pere the cook: tall, with carefully combed hair and his face a little scarred by smallpox, not much. My mistress always said he never overcharged and was an honest grocer and always gave fair weight. And that he wasn't a chatterbox.

Every day I felt more worn out. Lots of times I'd get back to the apartment and find the kids asleep. I spread a blanket on the dining-room floor with two pillows on it and I'd find them asleep, sometimes right next to each other and the boy with his arm around Rita. Till one day they weren't asleep and Rita, who was so tiny, was laughing, "Hee . . . hee . . . hee . . ." and they looked at each other and the boy put his finger to his lips and said, "Shut up." And Rita started laughing that laugh again, "Hee . . . hee . . . hee . . . ," a very strange laugh.

I wanted to find out what was going on, so one day I hurried home as fast as I could without stopping anywhere and I got there a little ahead of time. I opened the apartment door like a robber, holding my breath while I turned the key in the lock. The balcony was full of doves and there were some in the hallway too, and I couldn't see the children anywhere. As soon as I was in front of them three doves flew out the balcony doors, which were wide open, and got away, leaving a few feathers and their shadows. Four more made for the back porch as fast as they could, giving little hops from time to time and spreading their wings, and when they reached the porch they turned around to look at me and I waved my arms to scare them and they flew out. I started looking for the kids. I even looked under the beds, and I found them in that dark little room where we'd put Antoni when he was very small so he'd let us sleep Rita was sitting on the floor with a dove in her lap and the boy had three doves in front of him and was feeding them birdseed and they ate it right out of his hand. I said, "What's going on here?" and the doves were startled and started flying around, bumping into the walls. And the boy started crying with his hands on his head. And the trouble I had getting those doves out . . . and the act those kids had been putting on! I could see that for a while now the doves had been masters of the apartment in the mornings when I was away. They came in through the back porch, flew down the hall, and went out the balcony above the street and then back to the dovecote: a round trip. And that's how my children had learned to keep so still, so they wouldn't scare the doves and could have their company.

Quimet thought it was all very cute and he said the dovecote was the heart where the blood comes from that goes through the body and returns to the heart and how the doves left the dovecote which was the heart and went through the apartment which was the body and returned to the dovecote which was the heart. And he said we should try to get more doves, that they didn't cost anything or make any work. When the doves took off from the roof they rose up like a wave of lightning and wings and before they came back to roost they'd peck at the railings and the plaster on the walls, and near the railings you could see lots of patches of exposed brick. When Antoni walked through a flock of doves with Rita behind him the doves stayed calm as could be. Some made way for them and others followed them.

Quimet said that since the doves were used to the apartment, he'd put some nests in the little room. And when the children sat down on the roof they'd immediately be surrounded by doves who'd let themselves be touched. Quimet told Mateu he wanted to put nests in the little room. All they had to do was make a hole in the ceiling—a trapdoor he said—and the doves would have a shortcut to go back and forth between the dovecote and the apartment. Mateu said maybe the landlord wouldn't like it and Quimet said the landlord would never know and if we kept the doves clean he couldn't complain, and what he wanted was to keep raising more doves till he could go into business and let me and the children care for them. I told him he was crazy and he said women always want to give orders and he knew what he was doing. And no sooner said than done. Mateu, with his saintly patience, made a trapdoor and Quimet wanted to build a ladder but Mateu told him he'd get one from where he worked, that all he'd have to do was saw off one or two rungs because he thought it'd be a little too long.

And he set up some nests down below and for the time being he shut the door to the room so the pairs could get used to flying out the trapdoor instead of going through the apartment. The doves lived in darkness, because he also shut the trapdoor, which was made of boards. There was an iron ring on top so you could open it from the outside and from the inside we'd climb up the ladder and open it with our heads and shoulders. I couldn't kill even one chick because the children's shouts and tears would bring the house down. When I went into the little room to clean it I'd turn on the light and the doves would freeze and be dazzled. Cintet, with his mouth even more twisted than usual, got very mad.

"You're keeping those doves in jail."

And the doves locked in the dark laid eggs and sat on them and chicks hatched and when the chicks were covered with feathers Quimet opened the trapdoor and we watched through the little window he'd made in the door as the doves went up the ladder. They flew up one or two steps at a time. Quimet was overjoyed. He said we had room for eighty doves and if we sold the chicks from those eighty and got a good price he could start thinking about closing his shop and maybe buying a piece of property and Mateu could build him a house with leftovers from where he worked. When Quimet got home from work he'd eat his dinner without even looking at his plate and as soon as he'd finished he'd have me clear the table and start doing his accounts under that light with the strawberry-colored fringe: so many pairs of doves, so many chicks, so much birdseed, so much straw . . . and the final balance. I should mention that the doves took three or four days to get all the way up to the roof and that the ones up there welcomed them with pecks because they no longer recognized them. The one who got maddest was the white dove, the first one we'd found bleeding on the balcony. And when the doves on the roof had gotten completely used to the ones from down below, they went down to snoop around in the little room.

The house we were going to build had to be in the high

part of Barcelona, away from the center of town. Quimet would keep his doves in a special tower with a winding ramp that'd go all the way up to the top and the walls along the ramp would be lined with nests and there'd be a little window next to each nest and on top there'd be a terrace with a tile roof over it and spires, and the doves would take off from under the tiles and fly around Tibidabo Mountain and other places in the neighborhood. He said he was going to be famous for his doves because when he had his own house and didn't have to work in the shop any more he'd mix the breeds and one day he'd win a prize for dove breeding. But even so, since he enjoyed making furniture, he'd have Mateu build him a shed that he could use as a workshop and he'd make furniture just for his friends. Because he liked working and the only thing that annoyed him was having to deal with certain gentlemen who tried to cheat him, because there were some who were good people but there were so many who tried to cheat him that sometimes it took all the fun out of working. Whenever Mateu and Cintet came over they'd spend the whole time making plans, till one day Senyora Enriqueta told me Quimet gave away two out of every three pairs of doves, just for the pleasure of giving. . . . "And you, working away like an idiot. . . ."

All I heard was doves cooing. I was killing myself cleaning up after the doves. My whole body stank of doves. Doves on the roof, doves in the apartment. I'd see them in my dreams. The dove-girl. "We'll make a fountain," Cintet said, "with Colometa in the middle holding a dove in each hand." When I was walking through the streets on my way to work at my bosses' house, the sound of cooing followed me and buzzed in my brain like a bumblebee. Sometimes the lady spoke to me and I wouldn't answer her I was in such a daze, and she'd say, "Didn't you hear me?"

I couldn't tell her all I heard was doves, that my hands still smelled from the sulfur in the water dishes and the birdseed in the food trays. I couldn't tell her all I heard was doves crying for food with all the fury in their bodies made of dark flesh stuck full of quills. I couldn't tell her all I heard was doves cooing because I had them shut up in my house and that if I left the door open to that dovecote room the doves would scatter everywhere and keep flying out the balcony like some crazy game. And that it all began when I started working for her because I was so tired I didn't have the sense to say no when I needed to. I couldn't tell her I had no one to complain to, that it was my own private sickness and if I ever complained at home Quimet would start telling me his leg hurt. I couldn't tell her my children were like wildflowers no one took care of and my apartment, which used to be a heaven, had turned into a hell, and when I put the kids to bed at night and went "Ring, ring" on their belly buttons to make them laugh I heard doves cooing and my nose was full of the stench of feverish newly hatched doves.

I felt like all of me—my hair, my skin, my clothes—stank of doves. When no one was looking I'd smell my arms and sniff at my hair when I was combing it, and I didn't know how I could go on living with that stench of doves and chicks stuck in my nose and sometimes it just about knocked me over. Senyora Enriqueta put in her two cents' worth and told me I had no character, that she would have put an end to it by now and she'd never let anybody do something like that to her. Quimet's mother, whom I hardly ever saw because she'd suddenly gotten very old and weak and it was too much of a trip for her to come see us and I didn't have time to go see her on Sundays, showed up one day saying she wanted to see the doves, that when Quimet and the kids went to her house, which she complained wasn't very often, all they talked about was the doves and how they'd be rich before long and the boy told her how the doves followed him around and how he and Rita spoke to them like little brothers and sisters. She was shocked when she heard the doves cooing in the little room. She said only her son could have cooked up something like that. And she said she hadn't realized we kept them right inside the apartment. And I took her up to the roof and had her bend over in the shed and look down through the trapdoor and she got dizzy.

When she saw the sulfur in the water dishes she said you could only feed sulfur to chickens and it'd ruin the doves' livers. And while she was talking the doves were the bosses of the roof. They came and went, flew out of the little room and went back down into it, strutted along the railings and pecked at them with their beaks. They were like people. When they took off it was like a flight of light and shadow. They'd fly above our heads and their shadows fell on our faces. Quimet's mother tried to startle them, waving her arm like a windmill, but they didn't even look at her. The males strutted around the females: beaks out, beaks up, beaks down, tails out, sweeping the ground with the tips of their wings. They went in and out of the roosts and drank water and ate birdseed, their livers as calm as could be. When Quimet's mother recovered from her dizzy spell she wanted to see the roosts. The doves looked at us feverishly with their beady eyes. All their beaks were lined up, dark, with that fleshy pattern on them and pierced with two holes for the nose. The pouters looked like kings, the nuns were like soft, feathery balls, the turkeytails got a little nervous and left their nests and went outside.

"You want to see the eggs?" I asked her.

"No," Quimet's mother said. "Maybe they wouldn't want them afterwards. Doves are very jealous and don't like strangers."

Quimet's mother died just a week after that visit. One of her neighbors came to tell us early in the morning. I left the kids with Senyora Enriqueta and told her to do what she wanted with them and Quimet and I went to his mother's house. There was a big black bow tied to the door knocker and it fluttered in the bit of gray wind on that fall day that was just beginning. There were three ladies who were neighbors in her bedroom. They'd taken the bows off the bedposts and the top of the cross. They'd already dressed her. They'd put a black dress on her with a tulle collar with little spokes in it to hold it down and a strip of plush velvet around the bottom of the skirt. There was a very big wreath at the foot of the bed, made of green leaves with no flowers.

"Don't be surprised," said one of the women, who was very tall and kept moving her hands with long, thin fingers. "It's a flowerless wreath, just like she always wanted. My son's a gardener and she told him if she died before I did she wanted a flowerless wreath. It was her great dream . . . flowerless . . . flowerless, she always said. She said flowers were for little girls. And we used to talk about how if I died first she'd have a wreath made for me with flowers that were in season, that she wouldn't be dumb enough to have it made with strange flowers or flowers that were hard to find. Because for me a wreath with only leaves would be like having a big dinner without dessert. And as you see she was the first. . . ."

And Quimet said, "What do you want me to do about the wreath, since she's already got it?"

"If you want to, pay half. . . . That way we'll both have contributed."

And another neighbor spoke up. She had a harsh voice and said, "If my friend was trying to get something out of you she'd have her son make another wreath, because a hearse can be loaded with wreaths and in first-class funerals there's always an extra hearse to carry the wreaths that don't fit in the one in front."

"My son's specialty is wreaths and my friend knows all about it because he told her. . . . He also makes artificial wreaths."

And she said he made flowers out of beads that lasted a lifetime. He made flowers with beads: camellias, roses, blue lilies, daisies . . . flowers and leaves and little twisted branches, all very delicately colored. And the wires he strung the beads on never got rusty in the rain or in that damp air of death in the cemeteries. And the third lady said in a very sad voice: "She wanted a wreath of leaves. Neat and simple." And she said not many people died like she had: a saintly death. "She looks like a little girl." And as she looked at her she crossed her hands on her apron.

Quimet's mother was lying like a wax figure on the bedspread with red roses. She had her shoes off and they'd stuck her feet together with a big safety pin that went from one stocking to the other. They said they'd taken off her ring and the gold chain around her neck and they gave them to Quimet. And the neighbor whose son was a gardener said three or four days ago Quimet's mother had had some severe dizzy spells and she'd said they were like the one she'd had the day with the doves and they'd scared her and she didn't want to go out because she was afraid she'd fall down. And as the neighbor spoke she ran her hand through his mother's hair two or three times and said, "Doesn't she look nicely combed?" And she went on to say how last night when she was still alive you could see she'd been feeling sick and she'd gone to knock on the neighbor's door, and later she and her son had taken her home because when she tried to leave she found she couldn't stand up. And how between them she and her son had managed to get her into bed . . . She'd like to have her hair.

The lady with the harsh voice came over to the bed and stroked Quimet's mother's forehead and said that as soon as they realized her soul had taken flight they'd washed her hands and face and Father Elias was in time to make the sign of the holy cross over her. They said it had been easy to dress her because she'd been keeping everything all ready for a while now and she was always showing them the dress she kept hanging in her wardrobe on a cushioned hanger so the shoulders wouldn't get stretched out of shape. And she always told them that if she died and they dressed her not to put her shoes on because if it was true that dead people come back to the world she wanted to come back without anyone hearing her or bothering anyone. Quimet didn't know how to thank them, and the woman whose son was a gardener said, "A lot of people loved your mother. She was always running around like a puppy and happy to do you a favor. . . . Poor lady . . . Before we put her dress on we changed the ribbon on her medallion so she'll be able to introduce herself in heaven, if she hasn't already introduced herself, all neat and happy."

And the neighbor who'd talked least sat down and spread her skirts apart, holding them on each side with two fingers, and looked at us. After a while, since no one spoke, she said to Quimet: "Your mother loved you very much . . . and your children. But sometimes she told me it was her life's dream to have a little girl."

And the neighbor whose son was a gardener told her there were some things it was better not to say, especially at certain moments . . . that to tell a son who'd just lost his mother that she really wanted a girl didn't show much understanding. Quimet said they weren't telling him anything new because when he was little his mother to pretend would dress him like a girl and make him sleep in girls' nightgowns. And at that moment the neighbor who'd eaten with us the day of that saltless dinner came in without knocking. She was holding a little bunch of pansies and she said maybe it was time to call the funeral parlor.

Cintet and Quimet never stopped talking about the street patrols and how they'd have to be soldiers again and do whatever else was necessary. I told them fine, great, it was terrific to be in a street patrol but they'd already served in the army, and I told Cintet to stop bothering

Quimet and not get him all worked up about the patrols because we had enough headaches already. Cintet didn't look me in the eye for a week. And then one day he came to see me: "What's wrong with being in a patrol?"

I told him it was fine for some people, people like him who weren't married and if he wanted to join a patrol I didn't mind a bit but Quimet had enough to do at home and was too old. And he told me Quimet could get back in shape by going to Les Planes with him and working out there. And I said I didn't want Quimet in the patrols.

I was worn out. I was killing myself working and everything seemed to go wrong. Quimet didn't see that I needed a little help myself instead of spending all my time helping others and no one cared how I felt and everyone kept asking me to do more like I was superhuman. And Quimet kept bringing doves home and giving them away! And on Sundays he and Cintet would go off together. Even though he'd said he was going to put a sidecar on the motorcycle so we could all go on trips: him with the boy behind him and me with the girl in the sidecar. But like I said every Sunday he and Cintet would go off together. I guess they went to be in a patrol like they said they wanted to. Sometimes he still complained about his leg but he'd shut up quick because the boy would wrap a cloth around his leg and go hobbling around the dining room with Rita behind him with her arms raised. Quimet got mad and said I was raising the kids like gypsies.

One afternoon when the children were napping, someone knocked. Two knocks were for us; one knock for the people on the second floor. I went out on the landing to pull the cord. It was Mateu, and he shouted that he was coming up. As soon as I saw him I knew something was wrong. He sat down in the dining room and we started talking about the doves. He said his favorites were the ones with a kind of feathery hood behind their heads and their necks all purplish and green like a rainbow. He said a dove that didn't change colors like a rainbow was no dove at all. I asked him if he'd noticed how a lot of the ones with red legs also had black claws. And he said he wasn't interested in red legs and black claws; what set him thinking was the way they shimmered like rainbows. How come the doves shimmered green or purple according to which way the light hit them?

"I didn't tell Quimet, but a few days ago I met a gentleman who's got necktie doves."

I told him he'd done right not to say anything, because all I needed was for Quimet to bring home another kind of dove. And Mateu said the neckties were a band of curly feathers going down their breasts. The bands were like satin and the doves were called satin-tie doves. And he said, "If Quimet didn't have his mind on all this stuff that's going on he'd have heard about some doves with feathers that go up instead of down. They're called Chinese tie doves." And he said he knew it must be a pain to have to take care of so many doves and have them inside the apartment and that Quimet was a good lad but when he got mixed up in something . . . And when Quimet asked him to do something he couldn't say no, because Quimet had a way of looking him right in the eye that won him over . . . but he realized now that he never should have made that trapdoor. He asked how the kids were doing, and when I told him they were sleeping his face got so sad it scared me. . . . I told him the children and the doves were like one big family . . . kids and doves were all one. And how it all started when I had to leave them alone . . . And I went on talking but I felt like Mateu wasn't listening, that his mind had gone off and was paying a visit somewhere far away. Till finally I stopped talking, and when my voice stopped he found his and said he hadn't seen his daughter for a week because Griselda was working as a typist and had taken the girl to her parents' house and he couldn't live without the girl and knowing Griselda was seeing all kinds of people. . . . "And the girl away . . . and the girl away . . ." he kept saying as if he didn't know how to stop. Till finally he asked me to forgive him for coming to me with his troubles when a man has to know how to deal with them alone, but he knew me so well and for such a long time that I was like a sister to him and when he said I was like a sister he started crying and it scared me a lot. It was the first time I'd seen a man cry who was as tall as Saint Paul and had blue eyes. When he'd calmed down a little he tiptoed out so he wouldn't wake the children, and when he'd left something very strange stayed inside me: sadness mixed with a kind of sweet taste of feeling good that I'm not sure I ever felt before.

And I went up on the roof with the sky all billowed out and strawberry-colored at sunset and the doves flocking around my feet with their smooth feathers, those feathers the water flowed off when it rained without being able to get underneath. From time to time a light breeze ruffled the feathers on their necks. . . . Two or three took flight and they were black against the dark red sunset.

That night, instead of thinking about the doves and how tired I was, which sometimes kept me awake, I thought about Mateu's eyes which were the same color as the sea. The color of the sea when the sun was shining on it and Quimet and I went out on the motorcycle and without realizing I thought about things I understood but that I hadn't understood completely . . . or things I was learning and just beginning to find out about.

The next day I dropped a glass at my bosses' house and they made me pay for a new one even though it had been a little chipped. When I got home, loaded down with birdseed and so tired I could hardly stand up, I had to stop in front of those scales drawn on the wall, which was where I usually ran out of steam when I was tired. I slapped the boy a couple of times for no reason and he started to cry and when the girl saw him she started to cry too and that made three of us because I also started crying and the doves were cooing and when Quimet got home he found us all with tears streaming down our faces and said that was just what he needed.

"All morning long waxing furniture and plugging termite holes and when I come home instead of finding peace and happiness I find tears and drama and the pots still cold."

And he grabbed the kids under their arms and lifted them up high in the air and walked up and down the hall with one in each hand, and I told him to be careful or he'd break their arms and he said if they didn't stop crying he'd throw them out the window. And finally I choked back my tears and washed the kids' faces and washed my face and I didn't tell him I'd broken a glass and they'd taken it out of my pay because he was perfectly capable of going out looking for them and giving them hell.

And that was the day I told myself I'd had it. I'd had it with the doves. Doves, birdseed, water dishes, roosts, dovecote, ladder: the hell with them! But I didn't know how to go about it. And the thought burned in my head like a red-hot coal. And while Quimet was having breakfast with his legs wound around the legs of the chair and he unwound one and said maybe he had something like hot ashes on his knee and that was what made his bones burn, I was thinking about how to get rid of that village of doves and everything Quimet said went in one ear and out the other like there was a hole drilled between them.

I could feel that red-hot coal burning in my brain. Birdseed, water dishes, food trays, dovecote, baskets of dove droppings: out! Ladder, straw, bowls of sulfur, pouters, beady red eyes and red legs: out! Turkeytails, hoods, nuns, chicks and grownups: out! The roof shed mine, the trapdoor shut, the chairs in the shed, no more circling doves, the hamper on the roof, the clothes hung out to dry on the roof. Round eyes and sharp beaks, the mallow-rose rainbow and apple rainbow: out! Without meaning to, Quimet's mother had given me the solution. . . . And I started bothering the doves while they were roosting. I took advantage of the children's afternoon nap to go up on the roof and torture the doves. The roof shed was hot as an oven. All morning long the sun beat down on the roof and set it on fire. And between the doves' heat and the stench of their heat, it was like hell.

When they saw me coming the doves who were roosting raised their heads and stretched their necks. They spread their wings and tried to protect the nests. When I stuck my hand under their breasts they'd try and peck me. Some of them puffed up their feathers and wouldn't move, others ran away and watched nervously till I left so they could go back to their nests. Dove eggs are pretty, much prettier than chicken eggs. They fit right in your hand. I picked up the eggs under a dove who hadn't run away and I waved them in front of her beak and the dove, who didn't know a thing about hands or eggs or anything else, stretched her neck and opened her beak and tried to peck me. The eggs were small and shiny and warm from being covered by feathers and they smelled like feathers. After a while there were a lot of empty nests. And the eggs quietly rotting away in the straw. They rotted with half-formed chicks inside, all blood and yolk and their hearts the first thing.

Then I went back down to the apartment and into the little room. One dove flew out the trapdoor like a shriek. A little later she stuck her head out one side and watched me. The pouters wobbled off their nests and sat on the floor looking very worried. The turkeytails fought back the hardest. I rested for a few days and it was like nothing had happened. I had to get it over with. So instead of bothering the doves so they wouldn't want their chicks, I started taking the eggs and shaking them as hard as I could. I hoped they had chicks inside and their heads were smashing against the shells. Doves roost for eighteen days. When it was half over, I'd shake the eggs. The longer they'd been sitting on them the nastier they'd get. More fever. They'd try harder to peck me. When I stuck my hand under their hot feathers the doves' heads and beaks groped for my hand among the feathers and when my hand came out with the eggs they'd peck at it.

I slept badly all that time. I'd start in my sleep like when I was little and my parents quarreled and afterwards my mother would be sad and tired and sulk in corners. And I'd wake up in the middle of the night feeling like someone had tied a rope around my guts and was tugging on them, like I still had that cord on my belly button from when I was born and they were tugging all of me out through my belly button and as they tugged everything went out: my eyes and hands and nails and feet and my heart with that tube down the middle with a drop of black blood caught there and my toes still alive but feeling like they were dead . . . it was that same feeling. Everything sucked out into nothingness again through that little tube that had dried out after they knotted it. And all around that tugging which was taking me away there was a soft cloud of dove feathers so no one would see what was happening. It lasted for months. Months and months of bad dreams and messing up the doves' eggs. Lots of them kept on roosting two or three days longer than they were supposed to, waiting.

And after a few months Quimet started grumbling and said the doves weren't worth a penny and all they were good for was picking up bits of straw in their beaks and making nests and altogether it was a pain in the ass. All just because that's how it was.

All because I couldn't stand it any longer, with the kids locked up, washing dishes in that house where no one was any good for anything except to stuff spoonfuls of food down their throats, with that kid who'd turned out so skinny in spite of everything they did to make him strong. . . . And there were still doves cooing on the roof.

And while I was working on the great revolution with the doves the war started and everyone thought it was going to be over quickly. For a while we didn't have any gas. I mean it didn't get up to our apartment or down to my bosses' basement. The first day we had to cook lunch on a gray clay stove held together with metal strips, using charcoal I had to go out hunting for though I was almost too tired to walk.

"That's the last of it," the charcoal seller said, because her husband was in the street fighting. Quimet was mixed up in it too and every time he went out I thought maybe one day he wouldn't come back. He put on a blue work suit, and after a few days of smoke and churches with sparks flying out of them he came back with a revolver in his belt and a double-barreled shotgun over his shoulder. And it was hot, very hot. The clothes stuck to your back and the sheets stuck to your whole body and people were scared. After a few days the grocery store downstairs was empty and everyone talked about the same thing and how this business of a nation in arms always happened in the summer which was when people's blood boiled quicker. And how Africa must have melted away by now.

One day it was time for the milk to be delivered and they didn't bring it. And my bosses were all sitting in their dining room waiting for them to bring the milk. At twelve someone rang at the main gate and they told me to go open it, and the gentleman with the smock followed me. It was the milkman with his pushcart and he gave me two wax cartons and I took them. And the gentleman with the smock said, "Now you see how it is, eh? What did you think? Don't you see the poor can't get along without the rich?"

And the milkman closed his cart and asked the gentleman if he'd be kind enough to pay him—they usually paid by the week—since he didn't know if tomorrow he'd be able to bring more milk. The lady came up the stairs and heard what they were saying and asked what they'd done with the cows and said she hadn't thought the cows would be mixed up in the revolution and the milkman said, "No ma'am, I don't think they are . . . but everyone's out in the streets and we're going to close." "And how are we going to get along without milk?" the lady asked. And the gentleman got into it too and said, "When the workers try to be bosses they don't know the first thing about it. And tell me, do you want a revolution?" "No, sir," said the milkman. And he started pushing his cart up the hill without remembering he still hadn't been paid, and the gentleman stopped him and paid him and said he could see he was a good person even if he was a worker, and the milkman said, "I'm an old man now. . . ." And he went off pushing his cart and knocking on the doors to finish giving out the last cartons. I closed the gate and the daughter was waiting for us at the foot of the winding staircase and the lady, who was her mother, told her, "He says tomorrow there'll be no more milk." And the daughter said, "What'll we do?"

When we got to the dining room we all sat down and the gentleman told me how every night he listened to the radio and everything would be all right because they were already getting closer. And the next day, as soon as I'd unchained the door and set foot on the first step covered with soft dried-out jasmine flowers, I saw the lady. She was waiting for me next to the mimosa. Her face was covered with sweat and she sat down to rest.

"Last night they wanted to kill my husband."

"Who?" I said, and she said, "Let's go in the dining room. We'll be cooler there." And she said, "We were sitting in the wicker chairs yesterday at eight o'clock, the time my husband gets home from the office, and we heard him shouting, 'Come up! Come up!' from the front entrance. I went up. There was a militiaman behind him sticking a gun in his back."

"Why?" I asked.

"Wait," the lady said, laughing. "They thought he was a priest . . . since the top of his head's completely bald. . . . The militiaman thought he'd cut his hair to pretend and he brought my husband all the way from the Travessera with a gun in his back. And the militiaman said he was going to arrest him, and the trouble my husband had getting him to come home with him so he could show him his family. . . ."

I blushed for a second because I was afraid it was Quimet all worked up, but then I remembered that the lady knew him. But still it was a fright. And the lady said he'd told the militiaman they'd been married twenty-two years. And the militiaman left apologizing, and she said that night they'd all been glued to the radio and the lady's son-in-law, the gentleman with the smock, wouldn't let anyone else have the earphones and looked very worried as he was listening and said he couldn't hear a thing that night.

Two days after that joke with the militiaman, they rang at three in the afternoon. The lady went to open the gate, and as she was going down the marble stairs from the main entrance she got the shock of her life and her heart froze, because through the frosted glass with the little bubbles she saw a big crowd and above them some shadows that looked like sticks and were gun barrels.

She opened the door and six militiamen came in with a gentleman and a lady she knew and who'd owned an apartment house on Provença Street. It seems the gentleman in the smock had given them a mortgage on the building some years ago and since they hadn't paid the interest he'd taken over the building and now it was his. And the gentleman and the lady wanted it back, and they all went into the living room with the chest with Saint Eulalia on top of it, and the gentleman in the smock came upstairs and right away one of the militiamen, very slender and well built, made him sit down at the table and put a gun to his ear and told him to sign a piece of paper saying he was giving the building back to the owners. And how he'd stolen it from them. And how if they couldn't pay the interest it was because he charged them twelve percent and if they couldn't pay him he'd have to be good enough to wait. And the militiaman said, "Sign that paper right now saying you're giving the house back to these people. It's all they own."

And the lady said the gentleman was quiet as a mouse with the gun at his ear so he couldn't move his head and he didn't say a word and the militiaman got tired of not hearing him speak, and after a while the gentleman started saying very slowly and in a low voice that the gentleman and the lady were wrong and he hadn't done anything illegal and they told the militiaman, "Don't let him talk because if he talks he'll persuade you. He's capable of persuading Our Lord God himself."

And she said then the militiaman hit him with his gun and said, "Write!" and the gentleman became like a statue again. And everyone was getting tired but no one said a word and the gentleman, when they were all half asleep, started talking and he persuaded them, but first they took him to the committee. And he didn't come back till ten at night. He said all the revolutionaries had said he was right, but before they said he was right they'd taken him for a long ride in a car and in the trunk there were big kegs of alcohol to burn him in some deserted field. And he said he'd put on such a good act that the men from the committee had gotten mad at the people who'd lost the building for wasting their time when they had no time to waste. And while the lady was telling me all this a drop of sweat trickled down my back like a live snake.

And the next day another party. The lady was waiting for me at the foot of the stairs under that jasmine that was wilted from the heat. And she said, "They came last night at midnight. We never thought we'd get out alive."

They'd come and ransacked the house because of some tenants who painted revolvers on silk kerchiefs in a garage her son-in-law had rented them and because the tenants in a house that was also his and who didn't have a car had denounced him. But since the searchers had only found a lot of junk in the wardrobes and drawers, they'd left after making a list of everything. And the lady told me, "What those tenants wanted was for the militiamen to arrest us and make us live in their garage so they could come live in our house. What do you think the world's coming to?"

It got to be very hard to find birdseed and the doves started leaving.

Senyora Enriqueta said all that stuff was getting out of hand and ruining her business. They were turning everything upside down. And let's see how her bank account would end up. She started selling buttons and men's garters, sitting on the sidewalk on Pelayo Street. I hardly saw Quimet and it was a rare day that he came home to sleep. One day he told me things looked black and he'd have to go to the Aragonese front. And he said they'd been able to save Father Joan and how he'd crossed the border in a truck Cintet had gotten hold of dressed in some of Mateu's clothes. "Here," he said and gave me two gold coins. He told me Father Joan had given them to him for me and the children because we might need them even more than he did since for him, wherever he wound up God would look after him and wouldn't let him die before his time. I put the coins away and Quimet told me not to leave my bosses, that with all the time I'd been working for them they'd be able to help me out of a tight spot and that even if things looked black it'd be over soon and we'd just have to stick it out. And he said, "It seems Griselda's going out with some big shot and doesn't want to know anything about Mateu. . . . It's a shame."

He went off to Aragon and I went on working as usual. When I thought about things I felt like I was surrounded by wells and about to fall in one of them any minute. Then one day the gentleman with the smock gave me a little speech at one o'clock when I was about to go home.

"We're very pleased with you, and come see us any time you want to. But they've taken everything we had and no one pays us rent anymore. We know your husband's one of those rabble-rousers, and we'd rather not deal with people like that, you understand? We listen to the radio every night and that's what you all should be doing and then you'd realize you don't know what's going on and you're living in a dream world. Instead of waving flags you'd be better off making bandages because when they get done with you there won't be a single arm or leg left whole." And while he was saying this he paced up and down in the dining room and touched his Adam's apple from time to time. And he went on: "Don't think I'm saying anything against you. . . . It's just that we can't pay you. Right from the first day I've been telling you the poor can't live without the rich, and all those plasterers and locksmiths and cooks and bellhops who go driving around in big cars are going to pay for it with their blood."

And he stopped there. He went out to prop up the mimosa by the fountain. It was twisted like a worm and growing all crooked. Before I left the lady told me the company where her husband had worked for thirty years had been taken over by the clerks and he was helping run it. And again she said, "Whenever you want, you know . . ."

Quimet and Cintet dropped by at lunchtime, as if they'd just come out of the apartment downstairs, and Cintet told me he was in charge of a field gun and took it around from place to place. They'd come back from the front to see me and bring food and they left right away. The kids were sleeping, and before Quimet left he tiptoed into their room so he wouldn't wake them and kissed them. Mateu came by that same day, also wearing a militiaman's uniform and carrying a rifle. Very upset. I told him Quimet had been there a few hours before with Cintet and he said he wished he could have seen them. The sun kept shining and then clouding over and the dining room changed from yellow to white and back again. Mateu put his rifle down on the table. "You see what's become of us men of peace."

And he was very upset, at least as upset as Quimet and Cintet and me. And he said he'd only lived for two things: his work and his family, Griselda and the girl. And that he'd come to say goodbye because he was off to the front and how maybe God was sending him there to kill him off quicker because without Griselda and the girl he didn't have the heart to go on living. He sat there for a while, sometimes talking and sometimes silent. The children woke up and came out, and after they'd said hello to him they went out on the back porch to play marbles in the middle of a patch of sunlight that kept disappearing and then coming back again. And then, between a bright patch and a cloudy one, he asked me if I could give him something to remember me by because I was the only person he had in the world. I thought it over, but I couldn't think of anything someone could remember me by. And then I saw that little bunch of boxwood twigs that had been drying, tied with a red ribbon to a handle on the sideboard. I picked up the twigs and untied the ribbon and gave it to him and he took out his wallet and stuck it inside. And all of a sudden I got an urge to ask him something I'd never felt confident enough to ask . . . if he knew who Maria was . . . because Quimet sometimes mentioned her. . . . And he said he was sure Quimet had never known any girl named Maria. Never.

He said he was going and called the children and kissed them on the forehead, and when we were in front of the door and I was about to open it, he put his hand on mine and pushed it shut again and said he wanted to tell me something: that Quimet didn't know how lucky he was to have a wife like me and that he was telling me this at a moment when maybe we'd never see each other again so I'd remember it forever . . . the respect and affection he'd had for me ever since that first day when he'd come to fix up the kitchen. And I pretended and asked him why he was going away when deep down inside Griselda was a good girl and she'd realize how foolish she'd been and he said, "There's no other way. There's the thing with

Griselda but on top of that there's something even bigger that concerns everyone, because if we lose they'll wipe us off the map." He went out sadder than when he'd come in. I didn't see Quimet again for a long time and Senyora Enriqueta found me a job as a cleaning woman down at City Hall.

We were a crew, the clean-up crew. When I got into bed I'd touch the post I'd broken when Antoni was born and Quimet had grumbled so much about having to fix, and I'd touch the flowers that stuck up from the crocheted bedspread, and when I touched the post and the flowers in the dark I'd pretend everything was still the same and tomorrow morning I was going to get up and make breakfast for Quimet and Sunday we'd go see his mother and the boy was crying shut up in the room where we'd kept the doves and Rita wasn't born yet. And if I went further back I'd think about when I sold pastries in that shop full of glass and mirrors and nice smells and I wore a white uniform and could go out for walks.

And when I thought I'd never see Quimet again because he'd gone to war he came home one Sunday, covered with dust and loaded down with food. He put the packages on the table next to his revolver and rifle. He said they needed mattresses and he took away two of them: the boy's, since he said he could sleep with me, and the one on the brass bed I'd had when I was a girl. He said they had good trenches and sometimes they'd talk from one trench to the other with the soldiers on the other side but if you forgot yourself and stuck your head up they'd put a bullet through it and you'd be laid out dead. He said they had plenty to eat and everyone helped them and everyone was on their side and how lots of peasants had joined up and were swelling the ranks, but when they had to irrigate their fields or feed their animals they'd let them go home because they always came back afterwards. And how they spent days and days hanging around and never hearing a shot or talking with the men on the other side and sleeping all the time, and sleeping so much made it hard for him to sleep at night and he spent his nights watching the clouds and the stars and he never would have thought there were so many of them and so many different sizes when he'd been cooped up all day in his shop making furniture and more furniture.

And Antoni wanted to hear more about it and climbed up on his lap and made him show him how to shoot his revolver, and Quimet told him the war he was in wasn't like the others and it would be the last. It was like Antoni and Rita had fallen in love with their father and he told them next Sunday he'd bring them some Aragonese peasant dolls. We had a big lunch and afterwards he had to look for rope to tie up the mattresses and he went down to the grocer's shop. The grocer hadn't been very pleased with Quimet because he'd sent me to buy birdseed at another store. We called the grocer first from the back porch because he had the shutters down on his shop. He gave Quimet a long piece of rope, more than enough for what he needed, and he also gave him some empty sacks, and Quimet said the sacks would be perfect for making parapets. That he had a great idea for those sacks and they'd fill them with dirt and it would be perfect.

"You know, if I was your age," the grocer said, "instead of being an old man, I'd be out there fighting beside you.

I'd even enjoy it now that my store's empty. . . . War was different in my day. You probably know all about how they fought the Great War . . . nerve gas and everything." Quimet told him he knew all about the Great War because he'd collected stamps with generals on them that came in chocolate bars. "But the way young people make war now, it's a pleasure. . . . After all, once the first bit of bloodshed is over, this war can't go on much longer. . . . Like I said, it's a pleasure. And we'll have peace within a month. Take my word for it. What I don't agree with is the firing squads and executions and church burnings because they give us a bad name . . . but like I said, the way you all make war it's a pleasure and next time I'll have some more sacks for you and all you have to do is call down from the porch." And Quimet said he'd be back next week.

I told Quimet what had happened with my bosses and how I was working at City Hall and he said maybe it was better because working for the city I was doing some good. He looked in the little room, which didn't have any more doves in it, and I told him there were a few left on the roof: the oldest ones. They were half wild from hunger and I couldn't catch them or pick them up. He told me not to worry, that it didn't matter because everything in life had changed and would change even more and for the better and we'd all enjoy the results. He left at daybreak. On the side where the sun came up everything was red with blood. The horn on the truck that came to pick up Quimet would have woken the dead. Two militiamen came to carry the mattresses down and one told Quimet that Cintet had disappeared. He hadn't been there when they'd gone to his house and Quimet told him not to worry, that it was his fault for not telling them Cintet had gone to Cartagena to get banknotes and he wouldn't be back till the middle of the week.

Just three days after Quimet left, Cintet showed up wearing a very stiff new uniform with leather straps across the chest and back and a big basket of oranges. "For the kids," he said. He told me he'd been in Cartagena getting banknotes and the plane that took him there was very old and the wind lifted up the floorboards wherever they weren't weighted down and before they came in view of the city the pilot said that plane was such a jalopy that they might not get there flying and just as he was saying they might not get there, whoosh! a bird got in through a crack in the floor, blown in by the wind or sucked in by the vacuum and while they were concentrating on the bird and trying to get it out they arrived in Cartagena without worrying.

He took six cans of powdered milk and a package of coffee out of the knapsack he'd left on the table when he came in and he asked me to make him a cup of coffee and said what he missed most in all that martyrdom of war was eating off china plates and drinking coffee out of porcelain cups, and he said he'd get a kick out of drinking his coffee from one of those hot-chocolate cups that had made Quimet so mad, and we laughed. He said he'd brought me all those presents in memory of how fed up we'd gotten scraping wallpaper together. While I was heating the water for his coffee he said how sad he was that peaceful, happy people like us had gotten mixed up in a piece of history like that. And while he sipped his coffee he went on to say it was better to read about history in books than to make it with guns. I felt very surprised listening to him because I was seeing another Cintet, and I thought how war changes men.

When he'd finished his coffee he started talking again about his trip to Cartagena in the plane. He said it was something to tell his grandchildren about, that sometimes they'd seen fields of clouds beneath them and sometimes fields of blue sea, and he said when you look down at the sea it's all different colors with currents inside the water and how when the bird had gotten in he'd been swept into a corner because the wind was so strong it lifted up the floor and the bird and everything. And how the bird had lain there half dead with its belly up and pulling its claws in and a last drop of spit coming out of its beak and its eyes half glazed and half shut. And we started talking about Mateu. He said he and Quimet hadn't dared give Mateu advice because he was a little older than they were but how as soon as they met Griselda they said she was a doll and Mateu was too much man for a doll. And how Griselda would only give him problems. But some things you can't tell people and they have to be beaten into you.

Then he asked about the doves. I told him there were only a few left and they were half wild. I told him how every day I threw out a nest in the garbage, because the garbageman wouldn't have taken them all at once. I showed him the doves' room, which I'd cleaned a while ago. It still stank of doves. I'd closed off the trapdoor with some old cans up on the roof and the ladder was lying on the floor. He said, "When we've won I'll paint this room pink." I asked him when he'd be back and he said maybe he'd come next time Quimet came. He went down the stairs like a bolt of lightning and as he was going he called out, "Goodbye, goodbye. . . ." And he slammed the front door hard. I went back into the dining room, sat down at the table, and started digging old breadcrumbs out of a big crack in it. I did that for a while. Then someone rang and I went to the door and it was Senyora Enriqueta with the kids and they were very happy to see the oranges.

Early one morning when I was on my way to work I heard someone call out to me from a car that was going by. I turned around, the car stopped, and Julieta jumped out, looking very thin, her face white and her eyes feverish and tired. She asked how I was doing and I said fine and that Quimet was at the front in Aragon. She said she had lots of things to tell me and was I still living in the same apartment and how if I wanted to she'd like to spend Sunday afternoon with me. Before she got back in the car she told me they'd taken the pastryshop owner to the outskirts of town and shot him in the first days of the revolution because he'd had all kinds of hassles with his family, between one nephew he supported and another he wouldn't support because he was lazy, and this nephew had gotten him killed like he was a criminal and a traitor. And she told me she was in love with a guy who was also at the front and she got back in the car and I went on my way to work.

She came that Sunday. I'd been waiting for her since three o'clock. Senyora Enriqueta had come by to pick up the children and take them to her house because some people she knew had given her some cans of apricot jam and she'd serve them tea. I told her I had to stay because Julieta was coming to see me and she was in charge of the camps for refugee children from all over Spain. And

Senyora Enriqueta went off with the children and Julieta came and the first thing she said was how scared she was they'd kill her boyfriend and if he died she'd throw herself in the sea because she was very much in love, and how they'd slept together one night and nothing had happened. And that's why she was so much in love, because he was such a good person and she felt he loved her as few people know how to love.

They'd spent the night together in a house he was guarding because it had been taken over by his party. She said she'd arrived just as it was getting dark and it was October and when she'd pushed open the gate—shoving it hard because the last rainstorm had piled some sand up behind it—she'd found herself in a garden full of ivy and boxwood and cypresses and big trees and the wind blowing the leaves around and whap! a leaf hit her face like a ghost from the grave. And the house was surrounded by garden and between the shadows and the branches swaying and the house all shuttered and that wind and the leaves stirring and flying around, her heart was in her mouth. He'd said he'd meet her at the gate but that if he wasn't there she should go into the garden because it was better the neighbors didn't see her. And he was late and she stood there waiting while it got darker and darker and the cypresses shook all the time and swayed from side to side like the shadows of a whole crowd of dead people, those black cypresses you see in cemeteries. She said when he got there she was even more scared because she couldn't see his face and didn't know if it was him. And then they went inside and he followed her with a little flashlight, and it smelled like a haunted house and their footsteps echoed as if other people were walking in the other rooms and she thought maybe they were the ghosts of the people who'd owned the house who'd all been shot and she was terrified.

It was a house full of big rooms with curtains and wide balconies and high ceilings, and one room was lined with mirrors where you could see yourself from the front and back and sides, and their shadows danced and the light from the flashlight was all around them and a branch from a tree, flick, flack, tapped or brushed against the windowpanes according to how the wind felt like blowing. They found a closet full of evening gowns and fur coats, and she said she couldn't resist trying on one of the evening gowns, a black one with tulle that fluttered like a cloud and yellow roses on the blouse and skirt and it left her shoulders bare and he looked at her without daring to speak, and then they went out on a covered porch full of couches and pillows and lay down and embraced and listened to the wind blowing the leaves and moving the branches and that's how they spent the night: sometimes awake and sometimes sleeping, alone in the world with war and danger all around, and the moon came up and streaked everything with white wherever it came in through the slats in the shutters. It seemed like the first and last night, and they snuck out before daybreak and the whole garden was a battle between branches and wind and it seemed like the hanging ivy was alive and moving towards them and trying to touch their faces, and she took the evening gown with her because it didn't seem like stealing since the owners were dead, and she kept it in a box and when she got too lonely she'd put it on again for a while and close her eyes and hear the wind in that garden again—which wasn't like the wind anywhere else. And she said her boyfriend was tall and slender and his eyes were black and shiny like hard coal. And his lips were made to whisper to you and make you feel calm. And just from hearing his voice through his lips she saw the world differently. "If they kill him," she said, "if they kill him . . ."

I told her I wished I could spend a night like the one she'd spent so much in love, but I had work to do cleaning and dusting offices and taking care of the kids, and all those lovely things in life like the wind and the living ivy and the cypresses piercing the air and the leaves in the garden blowing from side to side weren't for me. That everything was over for me and all I could expect was sadness and headaches. She cheered me up and told me not to be so gloomy because the world was going to get better and everyone would be able to be happy because we were on this earth to be happy and not to suffer all the time. And that without the revolution a poor worker like her never could have spent a night of love like rich people. "And whatever happens, I'll always have that night! With the fear and everything and the leaves and the ivy and the streaks of moonlight and my man. . . ."

When I told Senyora Enriqueta about it she got very angry and said those girls in the revolution had no shame and since when did people spend the night with a boy in houses where the owners might have been shot, putting on gentlewomen's evening gowns to get him excited and stealing them in the end. She said there were some things you didn't do even as a joke. And she said the children had eaten a lot of jam, and while she was telling me about it they were standing on a chair in front of that picture of the lobsters with people's heads coming out of that smoky hole. I had a lot of trouble getting them down. And when the three of us were walking home with me in the middle and a child on each side, I don't know why but a drop of hot pain came up from deep inside me and stuck in my throat. And I stopped thinking about the garden and the ivy and the streaks of moonlight and made myself think about City Hall and called it a day.

All the lights were blue. It looked like the land of make believe and it was pretty. As soon as night fell, everything turned blue. They'd painted the glass on all the streetlights blue and when a crack of light showed in the window of some dark house, whistles would start blowing right away. And one time when the bombers came from the sea my father died. Not from a bomb but because he got so scared his heart stopped beating. It was hard for me to realize he was dead because for a while I'd felt like he was half dead . . . as if I'd never had anything to do with him or wanted to, as if when my mother died my father had died too. My father's wife came to tell me he was dead and to see if I could help her pay for the funeral. I gave her what I could, which wasn't much, and she left and for a moment, just a moment, standing in the middle of my dining room I saw myself as a little girl with a white ribbon on top of my head walking beside my father when he took my hand and we went down streets with gardens and we always walked down one street with big houses where there was a garden with a dog who'd throw himself against the bars and bark as we went by. For a moment I felt like I loved my father again or that once long ago I had loved him. I went to watch over the body and I could only stay two hours because I had to get up early the next morning and go clean the offices. And all you could say about my father's wife was that I never saw her again. I took away a picture of my father that my mother had worn all her life in a locket and when I showed it to the children they barely recognized him.

I hadn't heard anything from Quimet or Cintet or Mateu for a while. One Sunday Quimet showed up with seven militiamen, loaded with food and misery. Dirty and ragged and the others all the same. The seven of them left and said they'd pick him up tomorrow at daybreak. Quimet said they didn't have much food at the front because the organization wasn't working right and that he had tuberculosis. I asked him if a doctor had told him and he said he didn't need a doctor to tell him his lungs were all full of holes, and he didn't want to kiss the children because he was afraid of giving them his germs. I asked him if he could be cured and he said at his age when you catch one of these jokes you've got it for life, that when your lungs start collapsing and get like sieves and you're losing blood and it comes out your mouth because it doesn't know where else to go you can have your coffin made. And he said I didn't know how lucky I was to be in good health. . . .

I told him the doves had all flown away and there was only one left, one with half moons, skinny as a rail, who always came back. . . . And he said if it wasn't for the war he'd have a house by now and a tower for the doves with nests from top to bottom but he said everything would still turn out all right and how when they were on their way back they'd passed a lot of farmhouses where the people had loaded them up with food. He stayed three days because the next day the seven militiamen came back and said they'd been told to stay. And the three days he was with us Quimet never stopped talking about how there was no place in the world a person felt as good as he did at home and when the war was over he'd burrow into his house like a termite in a tree and they'd never get him out. And as he was talking he'd run his fingernail along the crack in the table and dig out breadcrumbs that had gotten stuck there, and it seemed strange to me that he'd do something I did sometimes but that he'd never seen me do.

During those few days he was with us he'd take a nap after lunch and the children would get into bed and sleep with him because since they didn't see him much they missed him a lot. I felt bad to have to leave every morning and go clean the offices. Quimet said those blue lights got on his nerves and if he was ever in charge he'd have all the lights painted red as if the whole country had the measles because he said he also knew a few jokes. And how the blue lights were useless: if they wanted to bomb they'd bomb even if the lights were painted black. I noticed how sunken his eyes had gotten, like they'd been nailed into his head. When he left he gave me a big hug. The children ate him up with kisses and went with him to the bottom of the stairs and so did I, and when we came back I stopped between the second floor landing and mine and ran my finger over the pans on the scales in the wall and the girl said her face hurt from her father's scratchy beard.

Senyora Enriqueta came to see me. When she knew Quimet was home she stayed away so as not to disturb us. She told me that for a few weeks now we'd been done for, that once they linked up we'd as good as lost and they'd as good as won and all they had to do was keep on pushing. And she said she was very concerned about us because if Quimet had kept quiet we wouldn't have had anything to worry about but the way he'd carried on who knew how it would end. I told the grocer downstairs what Senyora Enriqueta had said and he told me not to trust anyone and I told Senyora Enriqueta what the grocer downstairs had said and she said the grocer downstairs was praying we'd lose because with the war on he couldn't sell much even though he made a lot off a few under-the-counter deals in addition to the rationing. And how all the grocer downstairs wanted was for it to end one way or another but for it to end. And the grocer downstairs told me all Senyora Enriqueta thought about was the king and queen. And Julieta came to see me again and said old people were a pain and how they thought the opposite of us and what young people wanted was a healthy life. And she said some people think a healthy life is wicked and if you want to live a healthy life they jump on you like poisoned rats and arrest you and put you in jail.

I talked to her about the children and told her how every day we had less to eat and I didn't know how I could go on and if they switched Quimet to another front like he said they might I'd see him even less and he wouldn't be able to bring me the few things he brought, which were such a help. She told me she could get the boy into a camp, that she didn't recommend it for the girl because she was a girl, but that it'd even be good for the boy to get to know other little boys and it would help prepare him for life. And the boy, who was listening and holding onto my skirts, said he didn't want to leave even if he had nothing to eat. . . . But it was getting so hard to find food that I told him there was no other way, that it wouldn't be for long and that he'd enjoy playing with other little boys like himself.

I had two mouths to feed and nothing to put in them. I can't describe how sad it was. We went to bed early so we wouldn't notice we hadn't had supper. On Sundays we'd stay in bed all day so we wouldn't get so hungry. And we took the boy to the camp in a truck Julieta sent, after coaxing him into going. But he knew it was a trick. He knew it better than I did and I was the one who was playing the trick. And when we were talking about taking him to the camp before we took him there, he lowered his head and kept his mouth shut as if the grownups didn't exist. Senyora Enriqueta promised she'd go visit him. I told him I'd go every Sunday. The truck pulled out of Barcelona with us inside and a cardboard suitcase strapped to it and went down that dusty road that led to deception.

We went up a narrow stone staircase with very high steps and a ceiling over it and walls on each side and came out in a yard full of boys. Their heads were all shaved and covered with lumps and their faces were nothing but eyes. They were shouting and running around and when they saw us they gradually quieted down and stared at us like they'd never seen people before. A young teacher came up to us and showed us into her office and we had to cross the yard through that crowd of boys. She asked us what we wanted and Julieta showed her a piece of paper and said I had nothing to eat and how I wanted to leave the boy there because at least he'd be able to eat.

The teacher looked at him and asked him if he wanted to stay. He didn't say a word. Then she looked at me and I looked at her and I told her we'd made the trip to bring him to the camp and now that we'd brought him he'd have to stay. And the teacher looked me in the eye gently and said all those boys had just arrived but that maybe my son wouldn't fit in there. She looked at him again and I realized she was looking at him and that she saw what he was like: a flower. He'd made me suffer so much those first few months after he was born and I could hardly believe how handsome he'd become, with a wave of glossy black hair above his forehead and long eyelashes like a café singer. And skin as smooth as silk. Both of them, Antoni and Rita. They weren't like before the war, of course, but they were lovely.

I said I was going to leave him there and Julieta and I started walking toward the door, and the boy threw himself on me like a dying snake with tears pouring down his face and screaming not to leave him, that he wanted to stay at home, that he didn't like camps and not to leave him and not to leave him and not to leave him. And I had to harden my heart and push him away and I told him not to put on such an act because it wouldn't do him any good, that he had to stay and he would stay. That he'd like it there and make friends right away and play with the other boys and he said he'd already seen them, that they were bad and they'd beat him and he didn't want to stay. Julieta was softening but I stayed firm. And the teacher's forehead was covered with sweat and Rita, who was holding Julieta's hand, said she wanted Antoni.

Then I knelt down in front of the boy and explained to him very clearly that it couldn't be, that we had nothing to eat, that if he stayed at home we'd all die. That he'd only be there a little while, as long as it took for things to get better and they'd get better soon. . . . And he listened to me with his eyes lowered and his lips pursed and his hands hanging at his sides, and when I thought I'd convinced him we went to leave and he did the same thing. He ran after me and grabbed my skirts, "Don't leave me, don't leave me, don't leave me. I'll die and they'll beat me," and I said he wouldn't die and they wouldn't beat him and we ran out with me dragging the girl and Julieta in front of us and we ran through that cloud of boys with shaved heads and before we went down the stairs I turned around and I saw him on the other side of the yard holding the teacher's hand. He'd stopped crying and his face was like an old man's.

Julieta said she never could have done it and the driver, who was a friend of Julieta's, asked how it had gone and I told him and we drove back to Barcelona without talking as if we'd all committed some awful crime. When we were halfway there it started raining and the windshield wiper went from side to side, wiping and wiping, and the water ran down the windshield like a river of tears.

Senyora Enriqueta went to see the boy every Sunday and she always came back saying, "He's fine . . . he's fine. . . ." I didn't have time to go. Rita had a little more to eat but you could see in her eyes how much she missed Antoni and she wouldn't talk either. When I got home I'd find her where I left her. If it was dark she'd be out on the balcony. If the sirens had blown she'd be behind the front door with her lips trembling but not saying a word. Like a slap. Like ten slaps. Till one day a militiaman knocked on the door and told me Quimet and Cintet had died like men. And he gave me all that was left of Quimet: his watch.

And I went up on the roof to breathe. I went over to the railing above the street and stood there quietly for a while. It was windy. The clotheslines, rusty from not being used for so long, swayed from side to side, and the door to the shed kept slamming. I went to shut it. And inside, all the way in the back, there was a dove lying with his belly up, the one with the half moons. His neck feathers were still wet from his death sweat, his eyes were cloudy. Feathers and bones. I poked his feet, barely touching them with my finger. They were folded toward him, with the claws hanging down like hooks. He was already cold. And I left him there in what had been his home. And I shut the door. And I went back down to the apartment.

Sometimes I'd heard people say, "That person's like a cork," but I never understood what they meant. To me a cork was a stopper. If I couldn't get it back in the bottle after I'd opened it I'd trim it down with a knife. Like sharpening a pencil. And the cork would squeak. It was hard to cut because it wasn't hard or soft. And finally I understood what they meant when they said, "That person's like a cork. . . ." Because I was like a cork myself. Not because I was born that way but because I had to force myself to be. And to make my heart like stone. I had to be like a cork to keep going because if instead of being a cork with a heart of stone I'd been like before, made of flesh that hurts when you pinch it, I'd never have gotten across such a high, narrow, long bridge.

I put the watch in a drawer, thinking I'd give it to Antoni when he grew up. And I didn't want to think Quimet was dead. I wanted things to be like they'd always been: he was in the war and when it was over he'd come home with that pain in his leg and his lungs all full of holes and Cintet would come visit us with his eyes bulging out of his head, those eyes so still they seemed enchanted, and his mouth twisted. I'd wake up at night and all my insides were like a house when the moving men come and shift everything around. That's what I felt like inside: with wardrobes in the front hall and chairs with their legs sticking up and cups on the floor waiting to be wrapped in paper and packed in straw in boxes and the mattress and the bed taken apart and leaning against the wall and everything all messed up. I dressed in mourning as best I could. I wanted to do it for Quimet's sake since I hadn't for my father. I'd told myself everything was too mixed up for me to be worrying about things like dressing in mourning. And I walked through the streets that were dirty and sad in the daytime and dark and blue at night all dressed in black with my head on top like a white splotch that seemed to be getting smaller.

Griselda came to see me. To express her sympathies, she said. She had on snakeskin shoes with a matching purse and a white dress with red flowers on it. She said she'd been in touch with Mateu and things were okay between them because even though they each led separate lives they'd stayed friends for the girl's sake. That she'd never have thought Quimet and Cintet, who were just children, could have died. She was prettier than ever: more elegant, her skin whiter, her eyes greener and more liquid, calmer, like flowers that fold up and go to sleep at night. I told her the boy was in a camp for refugee children. She looked at me with those mint eyes and said she was sorry to hear it, that she wasn't saying it to worry me but that those camps were very sad.

And it was true. Griselda was right: those camps were very sad. When it came time for the boy to come home, Julieta went to get him. He was a different boy. They'd changed him. He'd swelled up and gotten chubby, with round cheeks and bony legs, roasted by the sun, his head shaved and covered with scabs, and with a big infected lump on his neck. He didn't even look at me. He went into the corner where he kept his toys and touched them with his fingertip like I'd done with the little claws on that dove with the half moons, and Rita said she hadn't messed up anything. And while the two of them were playing with the toys, Julieta and I looked at each other and we heard Rita telling him how his father had died in the war, how everyone died in the war and the war was something that killed everyone. She asked him if they'd heard the sirens at the camp. . . . Before she left Julieta said she'd try to bring me some powdered milk and canned meat. And that night for supper the three of us shared a sardine and a rotten tomato. And if we'd had a cat he wouldn't have gotten even the spine.

And we all slept together. Me in the middle and a child on each side. If we had to die we'd die together. And when there was an alarm during the night and the sirens woke us up we didn't say a word. We kept quiet, just listening, and when they sounded the all-clear we went back to sleep but we never knew who was sleeping because we always kept quiet.

The last winter was the saddest. They took sixteen-year-old boys. The walls were covered with posters and I—who hadn't understood the poster that said we had to make tanks and that had made Senyora Enriqueta and me laugh so hard—when I saw a scrap of it on some wall I didn't laugh anymore. There were old men drilling in the streets. Young and old, everyone to the war, and the war sucked them in and gave them death in return. Lots of tears, lots of sorrow inside and outside. Sometimes I thought about Mateu. I'd see him standing in the hallway as if he was real, so real it scared me, with his blue eyes, so much in love with Griselda and Griselda loved another. And Mateu's voice when he said they all had to go and how they all got caught there like rats in a trap. "There's no other way. There's no other way." Before selling Father Joan's two coins I sold everything else: the embroidered sheets, the good dishes, the silverware. . . . The women who worked with me at City Hall bought everything and made some money reselling it. I could barely buy food because I had almost no money and because there was no food to buy. The milk was milkless. They said the meat, when there was any, was horsemeat.

And people started leaving. The grocer downstairs said "Look, look at all those posters and newspapers. . . . It's time to get out." And the last day was windy and cold and the wind blew scraps of paper around and covered the street with white splotches. And it was always cold in my heart. How we made it through those days I don't know. Between when one bunch left and the others arrived I kept the apartment locked. Senyora Enriqueta brought me a few cans from a warehouse the neighbors had looted. Someone told me they were handing out food somewhere and I went there. I don't know. When I got home the grocer was standing in front of his shop and he didn't say hello to me. That afternoon I went to see Senyora Enriqueta and she said we'd taken a step forward and she was sure we'd have a king again. And she gave me half an escarole.

And we lived. We still went on living. And I didn't know anything about what was going on till one day Senyora Enriqueta came to tell me she knew for a fact that they'd shot Mateu in the middle of a square, and when I asked,

"In the middle of what square?" because I didn't know what else to say she said in the middle of a square but she didn't know which one. "Yes, yes, you can believe it. They're shooting them all in the middle of a square." And the hard pain didn't come up till five minutes later, and I whispered like my soul had just died in my heart: "Not that . . . not that. . . ." Because it couldn't be they'd shot Mateu in the middle of a square. It couldn't be! And Senyora Enriqueta said if she'd known I was going to take it so hard with all the blood gone from my face she wouldn't have said anything.

Without work, without anything in sight, I finished selling everything I had: the bed I'd had when I was a girl, the mattress from the bed with the columns, Quimet's watch that I'd wanted to give Antoni when he grew up. All my clothes. The wine glasses, the cups, the sideboard. . . . And when there was nothing left except those coins I felt were sacred, I swallowed my pride and went to see my old bosses.

Another streetcar had to stop short and let me cross the Carrer Gran. The driver yelled at me and I saw people laughing. I stopped in front of the shop with the oilcloth and pretended I was looking in the window, because to tell the truth I didn't see a thing: only patches of color, the dolls' shadows. The smell of old oilcloth came through the door and went up my nose and into my brain and confused it. The grocer with the birdseed had his shop open. A maid was sweeping the street in front of the boardinghouse on the corner and there were flowerpots again and a different color curtain in the bar. I went up to the garden gate and without thinking I started tugging on the lock to get the gate open, and it was hard. I'd always had trouble getting it open but now it was even harder. Finally I got it open a little and stuck my hand through the crack to unhook the chain . . . and suddenly I changed my mind and pulled my hand back and shut the gate again, which scraped along the ground, and I rang the bell. The gentleman with the smock came out on the porch right away. He looked at me and then disappeared because he was coming down to let me in.

"Well, what is it?"

He said, "What is it?" in a voice that sounded colder than a whiplash. I heard someone walking on the sand and it was the lady coming to see who'd rung. As soon as she got near the gentleman left us alone and went back upstairs. And the lady and I walked through the garden and stopped in front of the cement courtyard. The boy was inside the empty fountain and was scraping some green soapsuds with a trowel. He didn't recognize me. I told the lady I was looking for work and I'd thought maybe they—and the gentleman, who must have heard me, came out and said they didn't have any work and what made me think he was in a position to give anyone a job and how they'd lost a lot and had to make it back and as for the revolutionaries let them sink or swim! And he wasn't in the mood to stick his neck out and he wasn't running a poorhouse and they'd rather have their house dirty than have to deal with riffraff. The lady told him to calm down. She looked at me and said the war had wrecked his nerves and he got all worked up over nothing . . . but it was true they had to be careful with their money and if I didn't believe them look at the boy, poor thing, having to clean the fountain, and they weren't in any position to pay a maid. And when I told them Quimet had died in the war the gentleman said he was very sorry but he certainly hadn't made him go. And he called me a red and said, "You understand? We'd be sticking our necks out if we hired someone like you. It's not our fault."

And the lady walked me to the gate and when we were in front of the fountain in the wall she stopped and said he'd turned into a fascist—her son-in-law, she meant—because when they took him for that ride he seemed to be able to digest it, but afterward he never quite got it out of his system and instead he had a kind of constant heartburn and he made them suffer too. I went out into the street and helped her shut the gate, pushing it with my knee, and she said the wood was swollen from the rain and that's why the gate scraped on the ground. I stopped for a moment to catch my breath in front of the grocery shop with the birdseed. The shop was half empty and there were no sacks in the street. I walked on for a while and then stopped in front of the shop with the oilcloth to look at the dolls and a teddy bear with black velvet in his ears and black velvet overalls. He had a blue ribbon around his neck and black velvet on the tip of his nose. He looked at me. He was sitting at the feet of a very rich-looking doll. His eyes were orange with dark, shiny pupils like water in a well. And with his arms out and the white soles of his feet he looked like one of those dummies soldiers practice on. I was so fascinated I don't know how much time passed and suddenly I felt very tired, and just when I was going to cross the Carrer Gran and had one foot on the street and one on the curb, in the middle of the day and when they'd stopped having blue lights, I saw them. And I keeled over like a sack of potatoes. And when I was climbing the stairs to my apartment and I stopped for breath in front of the scales I couldn't remember what had happened to me. It was like I'd been dead from when I stepped into the street to when I got to the scales.

Senyora Enriqueta found me a job Saturdays cleaning the stairways in a building and two mornings a week I went to clean a movie house where they showed newsreels about everything that was happening in the world. But all together it was just a drop in the bucket. And one night when I was lying with Antoni on one side and Rita on the other, with their ribs sticking out and their bodies all lined with bright blue veins, I decided to kill them. I didn't know how I was going to do it. I couldn't blindfold them and throw them off the balcony. What if they only broke a leg? And they were stronger than I was. I had about as much strength as a dead cat. I couldn't do it. I fell asleep with my head splitting and my feet numb.

And then I saw those hands. The ceiling became soft like a cloud. The hands were cotton, boneless. And as they came down the light shone through them like my hands when I was a little girl and I held them up against the sun. And as they were coming down from the ceiling the hands which had been together pulled apart, and as they were coming down the children stopped being children and turned into eggs. And those hands picked up the children who were shells with yolks inside them and lifted them up very carefully and started shaking them. First slowly and then furiously, as if all the fury of the doves and the war and losing was inside those hands that were shaking my children. I wanted to scream but my voice wouldn't come out. I wanted to yell for the neighbors, for the cops, for someone to come and chase away those hands, but when my voice was about to come out I changed my mind and held it in because the cops would have arrested me because Quimet had died in the war.

I couldn't go on. I looked for the funnel. We hadn't eaten anything in two days. I'd sold Father Joan's two coins a while ago and when I sold them I felt like someone was pulling all my teeth out. Everything was over. Where was the funnel? Where had I put it? I was sure I hadn't sold it with the other stuff. Where was it, where? After lots of looking and turning everything upside down I finally found it lying on top of a kitchen cupboard. I was standing on a chair when I found it waiting for me, lying on its side all covered with dust. I picked it up and I don't know why but I washed it and put it away in the cupboard. All I had to do was buy some hydrochloric acid. When they were sleeping I'd stick the funnel in their mouths, first one and then the other, and pour the acid into them and then pour it into myself and that way we'd put an end to it all and everyone would be happy since we wouldn't have done anybody any harm and no one loved us.

I didn't have a cent to buy the acid. The grocer downstairs wouldn't even look at me and I don't think it was because he was a bad person but because he was scared after all the militiamen who'd come to our house. And like a flash I thought of the grocer who'd sold me birdseed. I'd go there with a bottle and ask for the acid and when it came time to pay I'd open my purse and say I left my money at home and I'd come by and pay him the next day. I went out for a walk without the purse or the bottle. I still couldn't bring myself to do it. The streetcars had screens instead of glass in the windows. People were badly dressed.

Everything was still recovering from the long illness. And I started walking. I looked at the people who didn't notice me and thought how they didn't know I was planning to kill my children, burning them up inside with hydrochloric acid. And without realizing what I was doing I started following a fat lady with a shawl who was carrying two candles tied together with a strip of newspaper around the middle. It was a calm, cloudy day. Whenever a ray of sunshine got through, the lady's shawl would sparkle and so would her coat, which was fly-colored like Father Joan's cassock. A gentleman coming the other way said hello to her and they stopped for a moment and I pretended to look in a shop window and I saw the lady's face in the glass and she had big jowls like a dog and the lady started crying and suddenly she raised her arm a little and showed the gentleman the candles and they shook hands and both went on their way and I started following the lady again because it kept me company to watch her and to watch her shawl fluttering a little on each side in the breeze she made walking.

The sun stayed hidden for a long time and everything got darker and darker and it started to rain. Before it started raining one sidewalk had been wet from the humidity and the other one dry. The rain quickly evened them up. The lady with the candles had an umbrella and she opened it and it got shiny right away and soon raindrops were running off the tips of the spokes. One drop kept falling in the middle of her back, like it was the same one each time, and they slid slowly downward. I was soaked. My hair got wetter and wetter and the lady kept on walking and walking like a beetle, stubborn and determined, with me behind her till she got to a church and closed her umbrella—which was a man's—and hung it over her arm. At that moment I saw a one-legged man coming toward me, and he stopped in front of me and asked me how I was and I couldn't figure out who he was even though I knew I recognized him, and he asked about my husband and told me he had his own shop now and how he'd fought in the war on the other side and had a much easier time now because of it. And I couldn't remember who he was for the life of me though I knew I recognized him, and he shook my hand and went away after telling me how sorry he was to hear my husband had died. And when he must have been fifty yards away I remembered, as if somebody'd whispered it in my ear. He was Quimet's old apprentice who'd been so little use to him.

And the lady with the man's umbrella and the candles was standing in front of the church hunting in her purse for some money to give a beggar woman dressed in rags with a half-dressed boy in her arms, and between the candles and the umbrella it was hard for the lady to get her purse open because a spoke had gotten caught in the fold of one of her pockets but she probably couldn't see it with the breeze blowing her shawl against one side of her face. When she'd given the woman something she went into the church through a little doorway and without knowing why I went in too.

The church was overflowing with people and the priest ran from side to side, with two altar boys helping him dressed in starched surplices with about a foot of embroidery on the bottom. The priest's chasuble was made of white silk with flowers stamped on it, all surrounded by gold strips and in the middle a cross made of light-colored jewels. And rays of red light came out from where the arms of the cross met. They were supposed to be light but they looked like blood. I walked slowly towards the main altar. I hadn't been in a church since the day I'd gotten married. Splotches of color came from the tall, thin windows, some of them with broken panes, that let you see bits of cloudy sky and the main altar was all covered with golden lilies with gold-leaf stems and leaves and it was like a scream of gold lifted upward by the pillars till it reached the spires on the roof, which gathered up the scream and sent it on to heaven. The lady with the man's umbrella lit the candles and fixed them in place and her hand trembled as she lit them.

When she finished she crossed herself and remained standing like me. Everyone else knelt down, and as I looked at them kneeling I forgot to kneel myself and the lady also remained standing up, maybe because she couldn't kneel, and they brought the incense around and as it spread I saw the little balls on top of the altar. A mountain of little balls a bit to one side in front of a bunch of golden lilies, and the mountain of little balls kept growing with new ones being born beside the others, very tightly packed and looking like soap bubbles all piled up one on top of the other and that mountain of little balls kept growing and maybe the priest saw them too because he opened his arms and put his hands on his head as if to say "Holy Virgin!" and I looked at the people and I turned around to look at the ones behind me and they all had their heads down and couldn't see the balls, so many of them that by now they were spilling off the altar and soon they'd reach the feet of the praying altar boys. And those balls that had started out looking like white grapes were slowly turning pink and then red. And they shone brighter and brighter. In the time it took me to close my eyes and rest them and try to figure out in the dark whether what I was seeing was real and then open them again, the balls became brighter. They looked like fish eggs, like those eggs in a little sac inside a fish that looks like the film around a child before he's born, and those balls were being born in the church like the church was the belly of some big fish. And if it went on much longer soon the whole church would be full of little balls and they'd cover the people and altars and pews.

And I began to hear some far-off voices, like they were coming from the great well of sorrows, like they were gurgling out of slit throats, out of lips that couldn't speak and the whole church was dead: the priest nailed to the altar with his silk chasuble and his bloody jeweled cross, the people spattered with the shadows of colors from those panes in the tall, thin windows. Nothing was alive: only the balls that kept spreading and had turned into blood with the smell of blood drowning out the smell of incense. Nothing but the smell of blood, which is the smell of death, and no one else saw what I saw because everyone had their heads down.

And above those far-off voices that I couldn't understand a chant of angels rose up, but it was a chant of angry angels who scolded the people and told them they were standing before the souls of all the soldiers who'd been killed in the war. And the chant told them to look at the evil that God made pour off the altar, that God was showing them the evil they'd done so they'd pray for it to end. And I saw the lady with the candles who also was standing up because she must not have been able to kneel and her eyes were popping out of her head and we looked at each other and stayed like that for a while as if we'd been turned to stone because she must have seen the dead soldiers too. She saw them too. Her eyes gave it away. They were the eyes of someone who's had somebody shot in the middle of a field. And frightened by that woman's eyes, I ran out half trampling the people who were kneeling and it was still raining outside like when I'd gone in. And everything was the same.

And I took off. Higher, higher, Colometa, fly, Colometa . . . with my face like a white blotch above the black of mourning . . . higher, Colometa, all the world's sorrow is behind you, get free of the world's sorrow, Colometa. Hurry, run. Run faster, don't let those bloody balls cut you off, don't let them trap you, fly, fly up the stairs, to the roof, to your dovecote . . . fly, Colometa. Fly, fly with your little round eyes and your beak with little nose-holes on top . . . and I ran home and everyone was dead. The dead ones and those who'd stayed alive. They might as well have been dead too and they acted like they'd been killed. And I ran up the stairs with the blood pounding in my head and cutting into my temples and I opened the door. I couldn't get the key in the lock and I closed the door and stood with my back to it, panting like I was drowning and I saw Mateu who took my hand and said there was no other way.

I went out carrying my purse—a little one just for change—and a basket with a bottle in it. I went down the stairs feeling like they were very long and ended in hell. They hadn't been painted in years and if you wore a black dress and brushed against the wall the dress would get white. The wall was covered with graffiti as high as your arm could reach: people and names, everything half rubbed out. The only clear thing was the scales because whoever drew them had carved them deep into the wall. The railing was sticky and damp. It had been raining all night. It was a winding staircase like the one in my bosses' house up to the first floor. Then from the second floor to mine it was made of red tiles with wood on the edges. I sat down on the steps. It was very early and you couldn't hear a sound. I looked at the bottle. It shone in the dim light on the staircase and I thought about the things I'd seen the day before and decided it must have been my weakness, and I thought how I'd like to bounce down the stairs like a ball, down and down and bam! the bottom. It was hard for me to get up. My hinges were rusty. "When your hinges get rusty," my mother used to say, "you can call it a day." I had a hard time getting up and I went down the winding part, clinging to the railing because I was scared I'd slip and fall.

The staircase stank of feathers. The smell came from a garbage can by the front door. There was a man poking through all the garbage cans. Running home the day before, I'd thought how maybe I could become a beggar. Do like that woman in front of the church who'd held out her hand to the lady with the man's umbrella. I could go out begging with the children . . . today one street, tomorrow another . . . today one church, tomorrow another . . . for the love of God . . . for the love of God. . . . The man looking through the garbage cans must have found something; he opened his sack and stuck whatever he'd found inside. There was a garbage can with wet sawdust at the top. Maybe there was something good underneath it like a crust of bread . . . but what's a crust of bread when you're starving? Even to eat grass you've got to have the strength to go out searching for it, and after all grass is nothing. . . . I'd learned to read and write and my mother'd gotten me used to wearing white clothes. I'd learned to read and write and I sold pastries and candy and chocolates and bonbons filled with liqueurs. And I could walk through the streets like a human being surrounded by other human beings. I'd learned to read and write and waited on people and helped them. . . .

A drop fell on me from a balcony, right on my nose. I crossed the Carrer Gran. A few stores were beginning to have some things in them and there were people in the street who went into those few stores and could afford to buy something. And I thought about those things to keep my mind busy so I couldn't think about that shiny green bottle in my basket. And I gazed at everything like I'd never seen it before; maybe because tomorrow I wouldn't be able to do any more gazing. It's not me looking, it's not me talking, it's not me seeing. Tomorrow nothing pretty or ugly would pass before my eyes. Now things were still there and they stayed there before my eyes like they wanted to fix themselves forever before I died. And my eyes were like windows taking it all in. The teddy bear wasn't in the oilcloth shop, and when I saw he wasn't there I realized how much I'd wanted to see him with his velvet overalls, sitting like a soldiers' dummy. . . . The smell of feathers in the garbage can by the front door had stayed in my nose and now it mixed with the smell of oilcloth and I walked on with the two smells in my nose till I passed the perfume shop, and then a wave of soap and good cologne came through the door.

I was getting closer to the grocer's shop. There were no sacks in the street. In my old bosses' house the lady would be making breakfast now while the boy played skittles in the courtyard. The basement walls would be soaked from the rain and those patches of mildew that glittered like salt would have gotten bigger. The grocer was standing behind the counter. There were two maids and a lady. I thought I'd seen one of the maids before. The grocer waited on the two maids and the lady, and my legs hurt from standing up. When it was my turn another maid came in. I put the bottle on the counter and said: "Hydrochloric acid." And when it came time to pay and a little smoke was still coming from between the glass and the stopper I opened my purse and acted surprised and said I'd left my money at home. The grocer said not to worry or make a special trip to pay him, that I could pay him some day when I happened to be passing by and it was convenient. He asked me how my bosses were and I told him it had been years since I'd worked there, ever since the beginning of the war, and he said he'd been in the war too and it was a miracle that he still had his shop, and he came out from behind the counter and put the bottle of acid in my basket.

I breathed a sigh of relief. And I left. I had to be careful that I didn't fall or get run over by a streetcar, especially the ones going toward town, and that I kept my head and went straight home without seeing any blue lights. Especially without seeing any blue lights. And I looked in the perfume shop window again, full of cologne bottles and shiny new nail scissors and little mascara cases with mirrors on top and little black tablets and brushes to paint your eyelashes.

And then the oilcloth shop again and the dolls with patent leather shoes . . . above all not to see the blue lights and to cross the streets without hurrying . . . not to see the blue lights . . . and then someone called out to me.

Someone called out to me and I turned around and it was the grocer and he came up behind me and when I turned around I thought of that woman who'd been changed to salt. And I thought the grocer was going to say he'd given me bleach instead of acid and I don't know what I thought. He asked me if I'd mind coming back with him to his store. That he was sorry to bother me but would I mind coming back with him to his store. And we went into the store and there was no one there and he asked me if I'd like to keep house for him, that he'd known me for a while and that the woman who'd been working for him had stopped because she was too old and got tired. . . . And then someone came in and he said, "I'll be right with you," and he was standing in front of me waiting for an answer. And since I didn't say anything he asked me if I already had a job and couldn't leave it and I shook my head and said I didn't know what to do. He said if I didn't have a job he had a nice little apartment and it wouldn't be much work and he already knew I was reliable. I nodded my head and he said, "Start tomorrow," and he went inside and got two cans of food and nervously stuck them in my basket along with a little bag of something. And he said I could start work tomorrow at nine. And without realizing what I was doing I took the bottle of acid out of my basket and carefully placed it on top of the counter. And I went out without a word. And when I got home, I—who'd always had a tough time crying—burst into tears like it was the simplest thing in the world.

There were flowers and acorns on the tablecloth and an inkspot in the middle. It was hidden by a brass vase with a string of ladies all around it dressed in nothing but veils with their hair flying loose behind them, and this vase was full of red roses and artificial daisies stuck in a clump of imitation moss. The tablecloth with the acorns and the spot in the middle had a fringe around it with three rows of knots along the bottom. The sideboard was reddish wood with pink marble on the top and a cupboard on the marble where he kept his glass. By glass I mean the wine glasses and a water pitcher and a fancy decanter for wine. A window that was always dark looked out on an airshaft. The kitchen window looked out on it too. The dining room had two windows and the other one looked into the shop, and that window was always open so he could see what was going on in the shop while he was in the dining room. The chairs had straw backs and seats with little holes in them. "You're not tired, are you?" the grocer would always ask me. His name was Antoni, the same as my son. I told him I was used to hard work and one day I told him I'd worked in a pastryshop when I was young. He liked talking to me from time to time. There was so little light in the dining room that you could hardly see his pockmarks. There was no door between the dining room and the shop. Just an opening to go in and out where the grocer had hung a reed curtain with a Japanese lady painted on it with a mountain of hair with needles sticking out and a fan in her hand with little faraway birds and nearby a burning lantern.

His house was simple and dark except for two rooms looking out on the street that led down to the market square. It was like this: there was a hallway leading from the curtain with the Japanese lady to the living room at the end, which had a couch and some easy chairs with slipcovers on them and a console table. To the left of the hallway were two doors next to each other that led into two bedrooms with windows facing the street that led to the market. To the right of the hallway was the kitchen and a little windowless storeroom full of bottles and sacks of grain and potatoes. And that's all for the hallway. At the end of the hallway was the living room; and to the right of the living room the grocer's bedroom, as big as the living room, with a balcony that opened onto a porch that was attached to the second-floor porch by four iron bars. You went out through this porch into a dusty courtyard separated from the second-floor garden by an iron fence.

This courtyard was always full of paper and bits of carpet sweepings from the upstairs apartments. There was only one tree in the second-floor garden: a stunted peach tree. The peaches would fall when they'd had time to get about as big as hazelnuts. And next to the bars on the second-floor garden there was a little gate with a grille he shut but didn't lock and which led to the street that led straight to the market square. Going back to the living room, there was a mirror on the console with carved wood on top of it. And two bell jars with country flowers: poppies, wheat stalks, cornflowers, wild roses. And between the two bell jars one of those seashells where you can hear the ocean when you put your ear to it. That shell with all the sea's moaning inside it was more to me than a person. No person could live with all those waves coming and going inside them. And whenever I dusted it I'd always pick it up and listen to it for a minute.

The floor tiles in his house were red. The kind that get dusty again the moment you finish scrubbing them. Onc of the first things the grocer told me was to be very careful not to leave the living room and bedroom balcony doors open too long because rats came in off the balconies. Little rats, with very long, thin feet. Humpbacked rats. They came out of the sewer grate in front of the barred gate to the courtyard and ran into the storeroom. They'd sneak in on the sly and gnaw the sacks and eat the grain. And it wouldn't have mattered so much that they ate the grain even though it was scarce if it wasn't for the fact that when he or his clerk went to get a sack and bring it to the store they'd drag it and all the grain would spill out and it was a nuisance to have to sweep it up. The clerk lived in the second-floor apartment. The grocer rented it to him because he didn't want strangers in his house once he'd pulled down the shutters.

The grocer slept in a double bed and later he explained to me that it had been his parents' bed and to him the bed smelled like his family, like his mother's hands when she made him baked apples at the beginning of winter. The bed was black with posts that started out thin, then got thicker, then thin again. They had knobs in the middle and then the second part began: thin and thicker and thin again. The bedspread was almost an identical twin of the one I'd owned and had to sell: all crocheted with roses on top and a fringe of crocheted curls you could wash and iron and either they wouldn't come uncurled at all or they'd immediately curl up again like they had a mind of their own. And there was a screen in one corner to get undressed behind.

It was hard for me to get back on my feet again, but slowly I returned to life after living in the pit of death. The children stopped looking like skeletons. And their veins didn't glow as fiercely. I slowly paid off the back rent, more with the money I saved than with what I earned because when it was time for me to leave the grocer always said, "Here." And he'd give me a little bag filled with bits of crumbled rice or small chick-peas. And he said he always wound up with a few more rations than he was supposed to have. The shop wasn't like it had been before the war, but it was a good shop . . . and he'd throw in a ham or bacon end to keep the dried beans company. Lots of stuff. Lots. I can't explain what it all meant to us. I'd leave his shop with my paper bags and hurry home and I always stopped to touch the scales and the children would be waiting for me wide-eyed: "What have you got?"

And I'd put the bags on the table and we'd sort through the dried beans and if they were lentils and there were stones, they'd bounce them on the floor and pick them up later and save them. And when it was nice out we'd go up on the roof at night and sit there with me in the middle and a child on each side, the same as when we slept. And sometimes when it was hot we'd fall asleep there and not get up till the sun turned us all red and woke us up, and we'd hurry downstairs with our eyes half shut so we wouldn't wake up completely and fall asleep again on a blanket because we didn't even have a mattress. And we'd sleep till it was time to get up and start another day. The children never mentioned their father, as if he'd never existed. And when I thought of him sometimes I'd make a big effort to stop myself because I couldn't describe how tired I felt inside and if I thought too much my brain would start aching like it was rotten inside.

After I'd been working a good while in the grocer's house, maybe thirteen months, maybe fifteen . . . leaving his house clean as a whistle month after month, with all the furniture oiled and the bedspread whiter than a lily and the slipcovers on the chairs and couch all washed and ironed time and time again, the grocer with the birdseed asked me one day if my children were in school, and I told him for the moment no. And one day he said he'd noticed me the first time I'd come in to buy birdseed, and he'd also noticed Quimet, "The guy who always waited outside," he said, "with his hands in his pockets and looking all around." I asked him how he could see him if he was waiting on me and he said, "Don't you remember how I left those sacks of birdseed out in the street? And even if I hadn't left them there and hadn't had to go outside to get the birdseed, I still would have seen him," because he said he had a mirror behind the counter that he'd put up so he could watch people and make sure they didn't steal anything. And how he could move the mirror from side to side and watch the sacks he'd left in the street and make sure the kids weren't sticking their hands in and pulling out birdseed.

And he said he hoped I wouldn't be annoyed, but the day he'd followed me to ask me if I'd like to work for him he'd run because the look on my face had scared the daylights out of him and he'd thought something awful must have happened to me. And I said nothing had happened. It was only that they'd killed Quimet in the war and times were tough and he said he'd been in the war too and spent a year in hospital. That they'd picked him up half ripped apart on the battlefield and pieced him back together as best they could and then he said, "Come over this Sunday at three." And he added that at his age he hoped it wouldn't bother me to be alone with him since I'd known him such a long time.

I touched the scales and went the rest of the way down the stairs. It was a half cloudy Sunday afternoon without sun or rain or a breeze. I had a little trouble breathing, like a fish when he's pulled out of the water. The grocer had told me to go in the courtyard gate, that it'd be open as usual because it was the only door he used on Sundays. He certainly wasn't going to waste his time raising and lowering the shutters when people came to visit. And I don't know why but even though I'd decided to go and was already on my way, I dawdled and wasted time looking at myself in all the shop windows and looked at myself walking by reflected in the windows where everything was dark and shiny. My hair kept getting in my face. I'd cut it myself and washed it and now it wouldn't stay put.

He was waiting for me, standing between two of the four bars that held up the back porches of the seven floors of his building. As I went in, a paper airplane came fluttering down from one of the top floors. The grocer caught it before it hit the ground and said it was better for him to keep his mouth shut because if he complained they might get mad and throw more stuff down. You could see he'd shaved a short while ago, and he'd cut himself a little near the ear. In that cloudy light the pockmarks on his skin seemed deeper. Each pock was round and the skin on them was newer and a little lighter than the skin you're born with.

He asked me if I'd like to come in. He made me walk in front of him and it felt strange because everything seemed different without the light that usually came through the reed curtain from the shop, and it looked like another house. He had the light on in the dining room. The light came from a porcelain bowl hanging upside down from six brass chains. There was a fringe of white glass tubes hanging from the bottom of the bowl and whenever anyone ran around upstairs they'd bump into each other and jingle. And we went into the dining room and sat down.

"Would you like some cookies?"

He put out a big square can filled to the top with layers and layers of vanilla wafers and he opened it and I said thanks but I wasn't a bit hungry. He asked me how the children were doing and while he was talking and putting the can back on the sideboard where he'd gotten it I realized that he was having a hard time saying and doing the things he said and did, and he seemed like a shellfish with its shell broken and all helpless. He asked me to excuse him for putting me to the trouble of coming there on a Sunday, that he was sure it must be the day I most needed to be at home so I could put things in order and spend some time with the children. And at that moment someone started running around upstairs and you could hear the glass on the light tinkling. . . . We both looked at the light, which was swaying back and forth, and when the glass stopped tinkling I asked him to tell me what was on his mind if by chance there was something he wanted to say.

And he put his hands together on the table with the fingers of one hand locked around the fingers on the other and when he'd squeezed them together so hard his knuckles were white he told me he was very worried. That he led a simple life, always shut up in his shop keeping things tidy and working all the time and cleaning and keeping an eye on the sacks in the storeroom so the rats wouldn't get into them because once a rat had made her nest in a bunch of dish-scrubbers and the rat had dirtied itself in them and he hadn't noticed even though he'd managed to kill the rat and her child and he'd put the dish-scrubbers on sale. And a maid who was always very nice to him but whom he didn't like at all bought two scrubbers, and a little later she came back with her mistress and the two of them cursed him out and said they couldn't believe he'd be so careless as to sell dish-scrubbers with rat filth inside. And how all that about the scrubbers was just one small detail to show me how careful he had to be that the rats who came out of the sewer didn't get into the courtyard.

He said his life wasn't much fun, that it wasn't a life to offer anyone like it was something grand, working all the time and trying to put something aside for his old age. He said he thought a lot about his old age and when he was old he wanted to be respected, and that old people are only respected if they have enough to live on. He said it wasn't that he wanted to deprive himself of anything he needed but he thought a lot about his old age and when he got to be toothless and bald and couldn't stand up straight and didn't have the strength to put his shoes on, he didn't want to find himself having to knock on the door to an old people's home and having to end his days there after a life devoted to hard work and struggle.

He unclasped his fingers and stuck two of them in the vase that covered the inkspot and picked up a bit of moss from among the roses and daisies and then without looking at me he said he'd always thought a lot about me and my children and he believed in people's destiny. . . .

And how he'd asked me to come that Sunday so we could talk calmly because there was something he had to ask me and he didn't know how to begin, mainly because he didn't know how I was going to take it. And they started running around again upstairs and the glass started tinkling again and he said, "As long as they don't cave in our ceiling. . . ." And he said it as if I was part of the household too. And he said he was alone. He was all alone, without parents or relatives of any kind. As alone as the rain. And how he was speaking to me in good faith and not to take what he was going to say wrong. . . . And he said he was all alone but he couldn't live that way. . . . And for a long time he was silent, and then he raised his head and looked me in the eye and said: "I'd like to get married but I can't start a family. . . ."

And he brought his fist down on the table as hard as he could. That's what he said: that he wanted to get married but he couldn't start a family. And he kept rolling the moss he'd taken from the brass vase into a little green ball. He got up and faced the Japanese lady and then turned around and sat down again, and as he was sitting down but hadn't really sat down yet he asked me:

"Will you marry me?"

I'd already been afraid of it, but even though I'd been afraid of it and I'd seen it coming I still was surprised and didn't completely understand.

"I'm free and so are you, and I need company and your children need someone to . . ."

He got up. He looked even more nervous than I was and he went through the reed curtain two or three times, going out of the dining room and coming back, going out and coming back. . . . And he sat down again and said I couldn't imagine how good he was. That I couldn't know how much goodness he had inside him. And how he'd always been fond of me ever since the first day I'd gone there to buy birdseed and he'd seen me leave so loaded down I could hardly walk.

"And when I think about you all by yourself and with the children shut up while you're working and how I could fix all that . . . If you don't want to, just pretend I never mentioned it. . . . But I have to tell you I can't start a family because my whole middle part was ruined in the war and with you, I'd have a family already made. And I don't want to fool anybody," he said, "Natalia."

I staggered up to my apartment like a drunken fly and even though I didn't want to go or say anything to anybody by ten o'clock I couldn't stand it any longer. I grabbed the kids and went flying over to Senyora Enriqueta's house, where I found her putting up her hair and getting ready for bed. I left the kids in front of the picture with the lobsters and told them to look at them, and Senyora Enriqueta and I shut ourselves up in the kitchen. I told her what had happened and how I felt like I understood it but I couldn't quite figure it out. And she said, "He must have been ruined in the war. It's just what you think it is and that's why he wants to marry you, because with you he'll have a ready-made family and without a family lots of men feel like an empty bottle adrift at sea."

"And how should I tell the kids about it?"

"Once you've said yes, just tell them like it's the most natural thing in the world. And what do they know . . ."

I thought it over for a few days and the day I finally

decided, after weighing all the pros and cons very carefully, I told the grocer yes, I'd marry him. I said I'd taken so long to tell him because he'd taken me by surprise and as time went on I'd gotten more surprised, and out of respect for the children who were older than their years because the war and hunger had made them grow up in a hurry. He took my hand and his hand was shaking and he told me I couldn't imagine how happy I'd made him. And I went to do my chores. I stood on the tiles streaked with sunlight and looked out the balcony. A shadow flew out of the peach tree: a bird. And a little cloud of dust fell into the courtyard from one of the back porches. I found a cobweb in the living room. It went from one bell jar to the other. It started from one of the wooden bases, then touched the tip of the seashell, and finally ended up on the wooden base of the other bell jar. And I looked around at what was going to be my home. And I felt a lump in my throat. Because as soon as I'd said yes I'd started feeling like I should have said no. Nothing pleased me: not the shop, or the hallway like a dark intestine, or the rats from the sewer. I told the children at lunchtime. Not exactly that I was getting married but that we were going to move to another house where a very kind gentleman would pay for their schooling. Neither of them said a word, though I think they understood. They'd gotten used to not speaking and their eyes had become sad.

And one morning three months after that Sunday, Antoni and I got married, and from that day on it was Antoni Sr. and Antoni Jr. till we got the idea of calling the boy Toni.

But before we were married he had the apartment fixed up. I said I wanted brass beds for the kids like the one I'd had when I was a girl and later had to sell and I got them. I said I wanted a pegboard with all new stuff for the kitchen and I got it. And one day I told him that even though I was poor I had sensitive feelings and I'd rather not bring even one wretched thing from my old apartment to the new one: not even clothes. And we got all new things, and when I said even though I was poor I had sensitive feelings he said he was the same. And it was true.

And the children began to study. Each one had a room with windows and golden beds with white bedspreads and yellow quilts in winter and night tables, and each one had an armchair. The day after we were married Antoni said he didn't want to see me working five minutes longer and I should look for a cleaning woman or a maid if I wanted one. How he hadn't married me to wash his clothes but to have a family like he'd said, and he wanted to see his family happy. We had everything. Clothes, dishes, silverware, perfumed soap. And since the bedrooms were freezing in winter and cold the rest of the year except for the middle of the summer, we all slept with footwarmers.

Senyora Enriqueta came to see me and the first time she came it was the same old story: trying to get me to tell her about my wedding night and what we'd looked like not being able to do anything. And she laughed. The first few times we sat next to each other on the couch but later we each sat in an armchair because she said the couch sagged too much and one of the ribs in her corset kept digging into the skin under her arm. She'd sit with her legs in a very funny position: her feet together and her knees spread apart, very straight-backed, with her mouth like a fish and her nose like a paper cone on top of everything. I showed her all the new stuff I had, the clothes and the linens, and she said Antoni couldn't have made all that money from his store, that he must have had some saved and I told her I didn't know. And she was amazed at the folding screen in our bedroom. "What an idea," she said. And when I told her I had a cleaning woman she said I deserved one. Her name was Rosa, and sometimes Senyora Enriqueta would come earlier to see Rosa, especially on her ironing day when she'd watch her iron in the living room. And starting the first day whenever she left Antoni would come out of the shop and give her a little bag of cookies, and he won her over so completely that when she came all she talked about was Antoni and she looked at him more lovingly than if he was her own husband.

One day we caught a very small rat. We found it after lunch, in a trap. I was the one who noticed it. We caught it in one of those traps that snap shut and it had gotten caught right in the middle. It's skin had burst and a little bit of blood and guts was trickling out and on the bottom you could see the muzzle of a baby rat. It was very delicate looking: its color, its little fingers, and the white skin on its belly that wasn't really white but looked white because it was a lighter gray than the rest of its body. There were three flies buzzing around the blood. When we came nearer, one of them flew away like it was frightened but it came back right away and joined the others. They were all dark black, with red and blue juices like the devil Quimet had described and they were stuffing themselves on the dead animal like Quimet said the devil did when he dressed as a fly. But their faces were black and Quimet had said when the devil's disguised as a fly his face and feet are all lit up like flames. So people won't mistake him for a real fly. And when Antoni saw us all so fascinated he grabbed the rat and the trap and went out in the street and threw them down the sewer grate.

I'd been afraid the kids wouldn't take to Antoni but they were crazy about him. Especially the boy. The girl was another story. She kept to herself more. But when the boy didn't have any homework he'd follow Antoni around, and if Antoni told him to do something he'd hop to it happily. And when Antoni was reading his paper after dinner the boy would go over to him and snuggle up, pretending he wanted to read it too.

I stayed at home. I was scared of the street. As soon as I stuck my nose out the door the crowds and cars and buses and motorcycles made me dizzy. . . . I was scared of everything. I only felt good at home. It was hard, but slowly I got to feel like the apartment and the things in it were mine. The light and darkness. I got to know the light during the day and where the streaks of sunlight fell that came in through the bedroom and living-room balconies: when they were long and when they were short.

And the children had their First Communions. We all wore new clothes. Senyora Enriqueta came to help me dress the girl. As I was scrubbing her from top to bottom with cologne I said, "Look what good posture she has. . . ." And Senyora Enriqueta said, "A drop of oil would run straight down her back." And we dressed her and Senyora Enriqueta's mouth was full of pins while she pinned Rita's veil and wreath to her head. When she was all dressed she looked like a doll. We had a party at our house afterwards and when it was over I went to the girl's room and helped her get her clothes off, and while I was folding up her petticoats on the bed she said one of her girlfriends at school had had her First Communion that same morning and her father had been in the war and they'd said he was dead and two days ago he'd come back very sick but alive. And the reason they hadn't heard from him was that he'd been in jail far away and they hadn't let him write letters. . . . And I slowly turned around and I saw the girl looking at me, and as she looked I realized how much she'd changed while I was struggling to get used to my new life. Rita was Quimet. Those monkey eyes and that thing that's so hard to describe but it's all to make you suffer. And that's when the agony started and the sleeping badly and not being able to sleep at all or even live.

If Quimet wasn't dead he'd come back. Who could tell me they'd seen him dead? No one. It's true the watch they'd brought me was his, but maybe it had gotten into someone else's hands and they'd thought he was dead because they'd found the watch on someone else's wrist. What if he was alive like Rita's friend's father and he came back sick and found me married to the grocer with the birdseed? It was the only thing I thought about. When the children were out and Antoni was waiting on people in the shop I'd pace up and down in the hallway like they'd made it just for me long before I knew I'd need it to pace up and down: from the living-room balcony to the Japanese lady in the dining room, from the Japanese lady to the living-room balcony. When I went in the boy's bedroom: a wall. When I went in the storeroom: a wall. Nothing but walls and the hallway and that reed curtain with the Japanese lady. Walls and walls and the hallway and walls and the hallway and me pacing up and down thinking about things and from time to time I'd go into one of the children's rooms like a hammer; and into the other one like a hammer and up and down and those walls. And opening and closing drawers. When the cleaning woman had finished washing the dishes and was going out and said in her fake-sweet voice, "See you tomorrow, Senyora Natalia," I'd go in the kitchen. And the wall. And the faucet. And I'd turn on the faucet so just a trickle would come out and cut through the trickle with my finger from side to side like a windshield wiper. And I'd stay there half an hour, three quarters of an hour, an hour . . . and finally I wouldn't even know what I was doing.

Till my arm started aching and kept me from thinking about Quimet coming home from some faraway land, maybe just getting out of jail and coming straight home and climbing the stairs to his apartment. And finding strangers in his house and going downstairs to ask the grocer what had happened and the grocer downstairs telling him I'd married the grocer with the birdseed because we all thought he was dead and he'd show up and wreck everything. And after fighting in the war he'd find himself with no home, no wife, and no children. Just out of jail. He'd come back sicker than ever. . . . Because I always believed him when he said he was sick. And if a slight breeze moved the reeds on the curtain with the Japanese lady and I had my back to the reeds I'd turn around frightened and worn out, thinking it was him. And how I'd try to follow him around explaining that it was nothing, that I'd only been married to him. . . . And he'd give me a couple of whacks that'd leave me flattened. And this fear lasted two or three years. Maybe more, maybe less, because some things get blurred in your mind . . . and Senyora Enriqueta got in the habit of talking about Quimet whenever we were alone together. "Remember how he used to take the boy out for rides on his motorcycle? And what he said when the boy was born and what he said when Rita was born and what he said when he called you Colometa? Remember? Remember?"

I had to get out of that apartment because I couldn't eat or sleep. I had to take walks. I had to think about other things. Everyone said I needed some fresh air. Because I lived like I was shut up in jail. The first time I went out with Rita after being shut up so many months, the smell in the streets made me dizzy. We went window-shopping on the Carrer Gran. We walked very slowly and when we got there Rita told me my eyes were terrified. And I told her I'd gotten a little crazy. And we looked in the windows and I couldn't have cared less. . . . And when we'd walked to the bottom Rita wanted to cross over and go up the other side, and when I stepped onto the edge of the curb everything got dark and I saw the blue lights, a good dozen of them at least, like a sea of blue spots swaying in front of my eyes. And I fell down. And they had to carry me home. When we were eating supper that night and I felt a little better Rita said, "I don't know what we're going to do. When she's about to cross the street, she faints." And she said my eyes got frightened. And everyone said it was because I'd stayed at home so long but I had to make an effort and slowly start going out more. And I did go out, but in different directions. And I went to parks all by myself. . . .

I saw lots of leaves fall and buds come out. One day when we were having lunch Rita went and said she only wanted to study languages so she could work for an airline. One of those ladies who help the passengers fasten their seat belts so they won't fly up in the air and bring them drinks and stick pillows behind their heads. And as soon as Rita opened her mouth Antoni said it sounded fine. And that night I told Antoni that before he said yes he should have talked it over with me and considered whether it was a good idea to work on a plane, and he said maybe it would have been better to talk it over first but if Rita had her heart set on flying we wouldn't be able to stop her even if we warned her a thousand times. And he said you have to leave young people alone because they think ahead even less than old people do. And he said he'd wanted to tell me something for a long time, and if he hadn't told me yet it was because I seemed like someone who didn't have much urge to talk or listen, but since we were already talking about Rita he wanted to tell me he'd never been so happy in his whole life as he was now that he had the three of us in his house, and he wanted to thank me because he felt lucky to be so happy and things were going well for him even if they weren't like before. And all the money he made was for us. And he fell asleep.

And I didn't know if I was sleeping or awake but I saw the doves. I saw them like before. Everything was the same: the dovecote painted dark blue, the nests full of straw, the roof with the wires getting rusty because I couldn't hang the clothes up, the trapdoor, the procession of doves marching through the apartment taking little steps from the back porch to the balcony. . . . Everything was the same, but it was pretty. The doves never got dirty or had fleas; they just flew through the air like God's angels. They took off like a shriek of light and wings above the rooftops. . . . The chicks were born already covered with feathers, veinless, with no tubes bulging under their sad little necks, with heads and beaks the right size for their bodies. And their parents didn't keep stuffing food into them nervously and frantically and the little ones didn't gulp it down with desperate cries. And when an egg fell out of the nest it wouldn't get rotten. I took care of them, I changed the straw in their nests. The water in the drinking dishes didn't get cloudy even when it was hot.

And the next day I told all this to a lady who sat down next to me on a park bench in front of some roses. I told her I'd had forty doves . . . forty pairs of doves: eighty. . . . All kinds. Satin-tie doves and doves with feathers that went up like they'd been born in the land of everything-turned-upside-down . . . pouters and turkeytails . . . white and red and black and speckled . . . with hoods, with capes . . . with a lock of feathers from their heads to their beaks covering their eyes . . . with coffee-colored half moons. . . . They all lived in a tower we'd made specially with a winding ramp, and alongside the ramp there were long, thin windows and inside under each window there was a nest with a dove roosting in it. And more doves on the windowsills waiting to take their places, and if you looked at the tower from far away it was like a big column all covered with doves that looked like they were carved from stone but were real. And how they never took off from the windows but only from the very top of the tower where they'd take flight like a garland of feathers and beaks but during the war a bomb had fallen and put an end to everything.

That lady must have told another lady about it. And the other lady must have told another. And gradually they all whispered it to each other and when they saw me coming one of them would always warn the others: "Here comes the dove lady." And sometimes one of them who still didn't know the story would ask: "And they all died in the war?" And another would say to her bench mate: "And she says she still thinks about them. . . ." And another would tell the ones who didn't know about it: "Her husband built a tower specially for her so she could fill it with doves and it looked like a heavenly cloud. . . ." And when they talked about what they thought I was like they'd say: "She misses her doves, the dove lady misses her doves, and all she does is long for them and for her tower with windows up to the very top."

And when I went to the parks I'd avoid the streets with too many cars on them because they'd make me dizzy and sometimes I'd have to go out of my way to keep on the side streets. And I had two or three ways to get to each park so I wouldn't get bored always going the same way. And I'd stop in front of the houses I liked and stare at them for a long time, and if I shut my eyes I could remember some of them by heart. And when I saw an open window with no one inside it I'd look in. And as I walked I'd be thinking: "I wonder if the window with the black piano will be open," or "I wonder if the window with the candle holder will be open," or "I wonder if the doorman in the building with the white marble entrance will be watering the potted plants in the street," or "I wonder if the house with the garden in front and the fountain with blue tiles will have the sprinkler going. . . ."

But on rainy days I stayed home and I'd get restless and finally I started going out on rainy days too, and there were no ladies in the park and I'd bring a newspaper and if it was just raining pitter-pat I'd spread the newspaper on a bench and open my umbrella and watch how the rain made the leaves droop and the flowers open or close . . . and I'd walk home and sometimes I'd get caught in a cloudburst but I didn't care, I even enjoyed it. I never was in a hurry to get home and if it was my day to go past the marble entrance with the potted plants out in the street so they could soak up the rain, I'd always stop and look at them for a while and I knew the leaves in each pot and which leaves had been trimmed to make room for the new ones. And I walked through the deserted streets and my life went very slowly. . . . And from always being around soft, gentle things I got to be sort of sappy and everything made me cry and I always carried a little handkerchief up my sleeve.

One evening when the boy was about to go to his room, Antoni told him to stay and sit with us for a while because he wanted to talk to him. I'd already cleared the table and put the tablecloth back on with the vase in the middle with the ring of ladies with veils and long hair. I'd changed the flowers a while ago because the roses and daisies had gotten faded and dirty and I'd replaced them with tulips and almond branches. Antoni asked the boy what he thought he'd like to be when he grew up, that since he was a good student and did well in school maybe he'd like to go in for some profession and he should start thinking what profession he'd like. That he should think it over calmly and not answer him right away because he had plenty of time.

The boy listened to him with his eyes lowered, and when Antoni stopped talking he raised his head and looked at me and then Antoni and said he didn't have to think it over because he'd already made up his mind a while ago. He said he didn't want a profession, that he studied so he'd know some of the things you have to know, because it was necessary to study and he was happy to do it because it gave him some polish, but he was practical and didn't want to leave home and all he wanted was to be a grocer like him because he said, "You're getting older every day and you're going to need more help." Antoni had picked up a little bit of moss and was rolling it into a ball. And he told the boy, "Well, this is how I see it: running a grocery is a job to keep from starving to death. But it's not something you can shine at."

And still kneading his little ball of moss, he went on to say that maybe Toni had said what he'd said just to make him happy and that he'd leave the subject open and let him think it over as much as he liked. He didn't want him to be sorry tomorrow that he'd tied himself down with some words he'd said to make someone else happy. And that he, Antoni, knew my son had a good enough head to be able to do whatever he wanted. The boy kept his lips pursed whenever he wasn't talking, and there were two long, stubborn wrinkles between his eyebrows. And he told Antoni he knew perfectly well what he was saying and doing and why he was saying and doing it. And he repeated this at least twice and finally he blew up—he, who was usually so obedient and reserved. He blew up but before he blew up he got nervous and grabbed a piece of moss and shook all the flowers and now they were both kneading their little balls. And he said he'd chosen to be a grocer because he wanted to help Antoni and carry on with what he was doing and help the shop expand because he liked that shop. He said good-night quickly and went to his room. And when we were going down the hallway single file Antoni kept saying as if he didn't know how to stop, "I don't deserve it . . . I don't deserve it . . ." but he also said he thought the boy was being foolish and that he would have been proud to see him a doctor or an architect and to think he was almost his own son.

We always got undressed behind the screen so we wouldn't have clothes scattered on the chairs and lying around the bedroom all night. There was a stool and some hooks behind the screen so we could take off our shoes and hang things up. Antoni would come out with his pajamas on and I'd come out before or after him in my nightgown, still buttoning up the front or the cuffs. At the beginning Antoni explained to me that he'd gotten the habit of undressing behind the screen from his mother. The cloth on the screen was crinkly and had some brass strips around it so you could take it off and wash it. It was sky blue, sprinkled with daisies like they'd been thrown onto it.

The nights when I slept lightly the first cart going to market would wake me up and I'd get up for a drink of water and drink it and listen to see if the children were sleeping well, and since I had nothing else to do I'd go through the reed curtain and walk around in the shop. I'd stick my hand in the sacks of grain. Mostly the one with corn because it was closest to the dining room. I'd stick my hand in and pull out a handful of little yellow kernels with white spots at the bottom and raise my hand and open it and all the kernels would rain down and I'd pick up another handful and afterwards I'd smell my hand and sniff all around. And in the glow from the kitchen where I'd left the light on, I saw the glass fronts on the drawers with little soup noodles inside: the stars, the alphabets, the pastina, the flakes. And the glass jars sparkled full of green olives and black olives all wrinkled like they'd been brought a hundred years ago. And I'd stir them with the wooden ladle that looked like an oar and the water would get foamy around the edges. And the smell of olives would come out.

And while I was busy with this I'd think how after all those years Quimet, who'd been like quicksilver designing furniture under the strawberry-colored fringe on the dining-room light, was really and truly dead . . . and I thought how I didn't know where he'd died or if they'd buried him, so far away . . . or if he was still lying on the ground among the dried grass of the Aragonese desert with his bones in the wind and the wind covering them with dust except for his ribs like an empty cage that had been an airpump full of pink lungs with deep holes in them and germs. And all his ribs were there except one which was me, and when I broke out of that rib cage I plucked a blue flower right away and pulled off the petals and they fell spinning through the air like those kernels of corn. And all the flowers were blue, the same color as the water in rivers and the sea and fountains, and all the leaves on the trees were green like that snake who was hiding with an apple in his huge mouth. And when I plucked the flower and pulled off the petals Adam slapped my hand: "Don't ruin everything!" And the snake couldn't laugh because he had to hang onto the apple and he snuck after me. . . . And I went back and turned off the light in the kitchen and the cart had gone by a while ago and more carts and trucks were coming, all going down and down and down . . . and sometimes all those wheels turning made my thoughts wander and I was able to get back to sleep.

"There's a young man here who wants to speak to you," Antoni said from the door to the living room. Rosa was ironing and I was sitting on the couch. He added that the young man had wanted to speak with him but he'd told him to wait a minute because it was me he had to speak to. It sounded a little odd. I told Rosa I'd be right back. "Okay, Senyora Natalia." I walked toward the dining room feeling quite curious, and when we were in the hallway Antoni told me the young man who wanted to speak to me was the nicest-looking guy in the neighborhood.

My legs felt like water by the time I got to the dining room. The owner of the bar on the corner was waiting for me there. He was almost like a new owner, because he'd bought it a little less than two years ago. Antoni was right. It made you feel good to look at him: very well built and with eyes as dark as a blackbird's wing. And very nice. As soon as he saw me he told me he was old fashioned. I asked him to have a seat and we sat down. Antoni left us alone, and he started talking. He said he had only one vice and that was work. "I'm a hard worker." He said he made enough from his bar and restaurant to live on and save some money but times had been bad and next year he was going to buy the soap shop next to his bar—they'd been discussing it for some time—and expand his bar and banquet room. And once he'd expanded them he'd make enough in three or four years to buy a little house near his parents' place in Cadaqués, because when he was married he wanted his wife to be able to spend her summers by the sea, which to him was one of the loveliest things on earth.

"My parents are very close. All I ever saw at home was joy and happiness. And when I'm married I want my wife to be able to say what I've always heard my mother say about my father: 'What luck, the day I bumped into him!' "

I listened to him without opening my mouth because he was like a windmill going full speed and I was waiting to see where he'd stop. And when he stopped talking, he stopped talking. And I waited and waited quite a while, and finally I broke the silence and said, "And you wanted to tell me . . ."

And there we were. Rita.

"Every time I see her go by it's like seeing a flower. And I've come to ask for her hand."

I got up and stuck my head through the reed curtain and called Antoni, and when he came in and I was going to tell him what we'd said, he said he already knew and sat down. I told him Rita hadn't said a word to me and I had to wait for my daughter to say something. And he said, "Call me Vicenç." And he added that Rita didn't know about it. I told him the first thing I had to do was talk it over with Rita but he should realize Rita was very young. He said he didn't care how young she was, that he'd wait if she wanted to wait but he was ready to get married the very next day and he didn't need to talk to her, he was old fashioned and wouldn't dare and we should talk to her and see what she said. "Ask around about me if you want to." I told him I'd speak to Rita but that my daughter had a bad temper and I wasn't sure we'd get anywhere that way. And no sooner said than done. When Rita came home I told her the boy from the bar had come to ask to marry her. She looked at me and instead of saying something she went to her room and put her books down and then went in the kitchen to wash her hands and came back and said: "You think I want to get married and bury myself being the corner coffee-seller's wife?"

She sat down in the dining room and brushed back her hair with both hands and her eyes were full of laughter, and all of a sudden she started laughing so hard she could hardly speak and once in a while when she could speak she said, "Don't make that face at me. . . ."

And I caught the laughter and without knowing why I started laughing too, and we laughed so hard that Antoni came and stuck his head through the reeds without coming into the dining room and said, "What's the joke?" And when we saw him we couldn't stop laughing and finally Rita said, "The joke's about getting married," and she told him she didn't want to get married, she wanted to travel and she didn't want to get married and we could tell the bar owner no and no and that he was wasting his time and she had other things to worry about. And she asked, "And he came himself to ask for me?" And Antoni said yes, and Rita broke up again, "Ha ha ha," and finally I said that was enough. It wasn't so funny that a nice boy like him wanted to marry her.

Antoni sent for Vicenç and when he came I told him, "Rita's headstrong and does what she wants," and how I was sorry to have to tell him. And he said, "Do you two want me?" We said yes and he said very formally, "Then Rita will be mine."

It started raining flowers in our house and we were invited to supper at the bar. Toni was on Rita's side and said he didn't like it at all, that she was right and why did she have to tie herself down to the guy in the corner bar when what she wanted to do was travel and if he wanted to get married the country was full of girls who'd kiss his hands out of gratitude.

One morning Rita was standing at the door to the back porch and I was doing something or other in the living room, and suddenly I saw her and stopped dead in my tracks in front of the balcony doors and looked at her. She was facing the courtyard and had her back to me and the sun cast her shadow across the floor, and her hair against the sun was full of shorter hairs all fluttering and sparkling and it made her look pretty. She was slender, with long, rounded legs, and she was drawing a line in the dust with her toe, slowly moving it from side to side.

Her foot went from side to side drawing the line, and all of a sudden I realized I was standing on Rita's shadow's head; or more precisely the shadow of her head fell a little above my feet, but even so I felt like Rita's shadow on the floor was a seesaw and I could go flying through the air any minute because Rita and the sun outside were heavier than me and the shadow inside. And I got a strong feeling of the passage of time. Not the time of clouds and sun and rain and the moving stars that adorn the night, not spring when its time comes or fall, not the time that makes leaves bud on branches and then tears them off or folds and unfolds and colors the flowers, but the time inside me, the time you can't see but it molds us. The time that rolls on and on in people's hearts and makes them roll along with it and gradually changes us inside and out and makes us what we'll be on our dying day. And while Rita was drawing that line in the dust with her toe, I saw her running around the dining room behind Toni or toddling through a cloud of doves. . . . And Rita turned around, a little startled to see me at the living-room door, and said she'd be right back and went out the courtyard gate. She came back a good half hour later. Her cheeks were burning and she said she'd just seen Vicenç and given him a piece of her mind because she told him the first thing a boy who wants to marry a girl has to do is win her heart and not hold secret conferences with her family, and she told him you don't send a girl flowers without knowing first whether she wants to get them. And I asked her what Vicenç had said and apparently he'd said he was crazy about her and if she wouldn't have him he'd close his bar and become a monk.

And we went to have supper at Vicenç's bar. Rita was wearing a blue dress with white polka dots embroidered on it. She acted annoyed the whole time and wouldn't taste even one course. She said she wasn't hungry. And finally when we were having dessert and the waiter had stopped bringing dishes and taking them away Vicenç said like he was talking to himself, "Some guys have a knack of making girls fall in love with them, and I guess I don't have it."

And he won her with those words. And their courtship began. A courtship like a war. Suddenly Rita would announce that she'd broken up with him and didn't want to marry Vicenç or anyone else. She'd shut herself in her room and only come out to go to class and as soon as she'd caught the bus, which stopped almost right in front of Vicenç's bar, he'd come over.

"Sometimes I think she loves me but then two days

later I think she doesn't. I give her a flower and she's happy, and two days later I give her another and she doesn't want it."

Antoni came into the dining room, sat down, and picked up his little bit of moss. He comforted Vicenç and told him that Rita was very young, just a puppy, and Vicenç said he took that into account and that's why he had so much patience, but it was wearing thin because with Rita he never knew where he stood. When it was time for Rita to come home Vicenç would make a quick getaway. Sometimes Toni joined the conversation, and when he saw how much Vicenç was suffering he got sad. Gradually he swung over to Vicenç's side and started arguing with Rita and defending him. "And when you've traveled around the world, what then?" he'd ask her.

When Antoni and the boy talked about the shop and what they needed and how to run the business I'd usually leave them alone or go in and out of the dining room without listening to them, straightening things up. But one night I heard the word "soldier," and I stopped at the kitchen door like I'd been nailed to the spot. And Antoni was telling him he was sure he could do his military service in Barcelona but he said something like he'd have to do an extra year, and the boy said he'd rather do an extra year and be in Barcelona than do a year less and end up God knows where. And he told Antoni not to be surprised, that when he was little during the war and we didn't have anything to eat he'd had to leave home for a while and it had left him with a kind of mad craving to be at home, to stay at home forever like a termite in a tree. And Antoni said, "I understand." And I went into the dining room and Antoni, who couldn't see my face, said soon I'd see my son in uniform.

Rita set the date for her wedding in front of everyone and said she was saying yes so she wouldn't have to see Vicenç any more looking like a soul in torment and getting the whole neighborhood on his side by making them think he was a victim. And just with that look on his face and without saying half a word making them think she was a bad girl. And with the reputation he was giving her if she didn't marry him she'd end up dressing saints, and she didn't want that either because now that she couldn't work on an airplane like she'd planned she wanted to be able to walk into a theater or a movie house all dressed up and with a handsome guy beside her and she realized that Vicenç was handsome. The only thing that bothered her, and it bothered her more than anything else, was that Vicenç was from the neighborhood and had his place so near where we lived. We asked her why that bothered her and she said she really didn't know how to explain it but it upset her to marry someone who lived so close because it was like marrying someone in the family and it killed a lot of her dreams.

And after they'd gone out together for a long time and had gotten to know each other, they started planning the wedding. Twice a week a dressmaker would come and turn our living room into a workroom. Vicenç would drop by while Rita and the dressmaker were sewing, and Rita would get nervous as soon as she saw him and said if he wasn't from the neighborhood he wouldn't be able to come snooping around. "He'll know what everything looks like ahead of time. . . ." Vicenç knew how Rita felt but he still couldn't keep himself from coming, and he'd go into the living room like he was committing a sin and stand there quietly for a while without moving, and when he saw us all working he'd go away and in the end I went away too and let Rita and the dressmaker finish because Rita decided I couldn't sew finely enough. So I went to the park, which made me tired. I was tired of all those ladies waiting for me with sorrowful looks on their faces because I'd had some doves. And as the years went by I'd gotten over that restlessness that made me want to talk about the doves and the tower.

I still liked to think about the doves sometimes but I preferred to think about them all by myself. And to think about them like I wanted to, because sometimes it made me sad and sometimes it didn't. And as I was sitting under the branches and leaves, some days I'd get the giggles because I saw myself years ago killing those chicks in their eggs. And when it was cloudy and I took my umbrella to the park and I saw a feather I'd push it deep into the ground with the point and bury it. And when I ran into one of the ladies who knew me and she said, "Aren't you coming over?" I'd say, "No. I don't know what it is, but I don't feel good sitting down." Or if it was cool out I'd say, "When I sit down all the water on the leaves drips down my back and I get coughing fits at night. . . ." And that's how I got rid of them and was able to enjoy myself looking at the trees with their heads underground eating dirt with their mouths and teeth which were the roots. And their blood flowed differently from people's blood: straight up the trunk from their heads to their feet. And the wind and the rain and the birds tickled the trees' feet that were born bright green and died bright yellow.

And I'd always come home feeling a little dizzy because

I don't know why but the air made me sick and then I'd go in the living room and find the light already on and Rita grumbling and the dressmaker looking worried and Vicenç standing or sitting around or he'd already left. And Antoni always asked me if I'd done much walking. And sometimes Toni watched the dressmaker and Rita sewing too, or I'd find him and Rita yelling at each other because he was hungry when he got home from the army and Rita didn't want to make him something because she said if she wasted time she wouldn't have everything ready for her wedding and she wanted everything finished so she'd never have to sew another stitch and could start just having fun as soon as she was married. Sometimes I'd find them all having tea and arguing about God knows what. And when I got home I'd go and take my shoes off and then sit down on the couch. And while they were talking I still could see the leaves, the living ones and the dead, some bursting forth like a groan and others falling without a word, whirling downward like tiny dove feathers that fall off in the air.

And the wedding came. It had rained all night and when it was time to go to church it was still coming down by the bucketful. Rita wore a regular wedding gown. I wanted her to wear one because in a good marriage the bride always wears a wedding gown. And at the same time Antoni and I celebrated our wedding anniversary. Senyora Enriqueta, who was getting old quickly, gave Rita the picture with the lobsters in it, "because you always stared at them when you were little. . . ." Antoni gave her a lot of money so she wouldn't be without a dowry. Vicenç said he was grateful but it really didn't matter because he'd have married Rita with or without a dowry and Rita said the dowry would come in handy when she got separated from Vicenç.

Rita's wedding had everything. The dinner was in the banquet room at Vicenç's bar, which he'd already enlarged because he'd bought the soap shop a while ago, and there were decorations hanging all around and wreaths of asparagus plants on the walls with white paper roses because the real ones were out of season. And ribbons hung down from the lights with paper roses tied to the bottoms and they also lit some red paper lanterns even though it was daytime. The waiters' shirts were so starched they could hardly move. Vicenç's parents came down from Cadaqués all dressed in black and with their shoes carefully polished and my children and Vicenç and Antoni all got me to have a gold silk dress made. And to wear a cultured pearl necklace.

Vicenç looked white as a sheet because the day had finally come after he'd said so often that it never would. He looked like he'd been killed and brought back to life. Rita was in a bad mood because her train and veil had gotten wet coming out of church. Toni couldn't make it to the church and came to the dinner wearing his uniform and he danced with it on. And we had to turn on the fans and the paper roses fluttered in the artificial breeze. And Rita danced with Antoni and Antoni looked as soft as a rotten peach. And Vicenç's parents, who'd never met me, said they were very pleased to make my acquaintance and I said I was very pleased to make theirs and they told me how in his letters Vicenç always talked about Rita and Senyora Natalia.

Rita took her veil off after the third dance because it was getting in her way and she danced with everybody, and as she danced she laughed and threw her head back and held up her skirts and her eyes sparkled and she had little drops of sweat between her nose and her upper lip. And when Rita danced with Antoni, Senyora Enriqueta, who was wearing earrings with lavender stones, came up to me and said, "If Quimet could see her now. . . ." And people I hardly knew came up to greet me and said, "How are you, Senyora Natalia. . . ." And when I danced with my son the soldier, pressing my palm with that whole span of wrinkled skin that goes from your wrist to your fingers against his palm, I felt like that bedpost made of wooden balls piled on top of each other was breaking and I dropped his hand and put my arm around his neck and squeezed it and he said, "What's up?" and I said, "I'm strangling you." And when the dance ended my cultured pearl necklace got caught on a button on his uniform and it broke and all the pearls spilled onto the floor and everyone started gathering them up and as they gathered them they gave them to me, "Here, here, Senyora Natalia," and I put them in my purse, "Here, here. . . ." I danced the waltz with Antoni, and everyone made a circle and watched us because before the music started Antoni had asked Vicenç to announce that we were celebrating our wedding anniversary.

And Rita came over and kissed me. While Vicenç was announcing the waltz she whispered to me that she'd fallen madly in love with him the first day but she didn't want to show it and Vicenç would never know how much she loved him. And her lips tickled when she said it and I felt her warm breath on my cheek for a moment. The party was breaking up and it was time to go home. Toni left, Rita gave out some flowers, and then the newlyweds left too. It had been so hot inside, and outside the evening was cool and pink and it felt like the end of summer. It had stopped raining but the whole street still smelled of rain.

Antoni and I walked home and went in the courtyard gate. I took my dress off behind the screen and Antoni said I ought to string the pearls on something stronger that wouldn't break, and he changed his clothes too and went to putter around in his shop. I sat down on the couch in front of the console table. I could see the top of my hair in the mirror on the console with those little flowers God knows how many years old on each side sleeping in their bell jars. The seashell was in the middle of the console, and I felt like I could hear the sea stirring inside it . . . booom . . . booom. . . . And I thought maybe it didn't make any noise when no one was listening and how no one would ever know if there were waves inside a seashell when nobody's ear was at the hole. I took the pearls out of my purse and put them in a little box and kept one and threw it in the seashell so it could keep the sea company.

I went to ask Antoni if he wanted anything for supper and he said, "Just coffee and milk, thanks." And he came into the dining room to talk to me because I'd called him from the hallway, and then he went back through the reeds into his shop and I went back to the couch till it got dark, and I sat there in the dark till the streetlights came on and a beam of pale light came in like the ghost of a light and streaked the red tiles. I picked up the seashell and very carefully turned it first one way and then the other so I could hear the pearl rolling around inside. It was tan with white spots and little spires and the spire on the end was worn away and there was mother-of-pearl inside. I put it back in its place and imagined the shell was a church and the pearl was Father Joan and the "Booom . . . booom . . ." was a chant sung by angels who only knew one song.

And I went back to the couch and sat there till Antoni came in and asked me what I was doing in the dark, and I told him I wasn't doing anything. And he asked if I was thinking about Rita and I said yes but I wasn't thinking about Rita. And he sat down beside me and said he'd like to go to bed early because he wasn't used to wearing armor and his body felt crushed, and I said I was tired too and we got up and I went to warm up the milk and make the coffee and he said, "Just half a cup for me. . . ."

Toni woke me up when he came home, even though when he came home at night he always tiptoed across the courtyard. I started running my finger along one of the crocheted flowers and tugging at a petal from time to time. A piece of furniture creaked, maybe the console, maybe the couch, maybe the chest of drawers . . . I saw the bottom of Rita's skirt again in the dark and how it whirled above her feet in their satin shoes with little diamond buckles. And the night went slowly. The roses on the bedspread had hearts in the middle and once one of the hearts wore through and half a button popped out from the middle, very small . . . Senyora Natalia.

I got up. Toni had left the balcony doors half open to keep from waking us. . . . I went to close them. But when I got there I turned around and went back in the bedroom and tiptoed behind the screen and got dressed. It was still dark out. I crept barefoot into the kitchen, touching the walls like I always did. I stopped in front of the boy's room and heard his strong, calm breathing. And by habit I went to get a drink of water. I opened the drawer in the white kitchen table with the checkered oilcloth cover and took out the paring knife with the sharp point.

The blade had little teeth like a saw . . . Senyora Natalia. Whoever invented that knife had done a good job and he must have worked on it a lot after supper under a light hanging over a table because knives used to be different back when they had to be sharpened and maybe the guy who'd burned the midnight oil inventing knives with serrated edges had put all the knife grinders out of business. Maybe the poor knife grinders had other jobs now and were making better money and had motorcycles and went tearing along the roads like lightning with their terrified wives behind them. Up and down the roads. Because everything was like that: roads and streets and hallways and houses you could burrow into like a termite in a trunk. Walls and more walls. Once in passing Quimet had said termites were a great misfortune, and I said I didn't understand how they could go on breathing always burrowing and burrowing and the more they burrowed the less they must have been able to breathe, and he said they were made to live with their noses in the wood and they were naturally hard workers. And I thought maybe the knife grinders could still make a living because not all the knives were in kitchens or camps and orphanages where the people in charge think about saving money and there were still knives with blades that needed sharpening on a grindstone.

And while I was thinking about all this the smells and stenches started. All of them. Chasing each other around, shoving each other out of the way and running away and coming back: the smell of the roof with the doves on it and the smell of the roof without the doves and the stench of bleach that I already knew when I got married. And the smell of blood like a warning of the smell of death. And the smell of sulfur in rockets and firecrackers that night in the Plaça del Diamant and the smell of paper flowers and the dry smell of asparagus plants crumbling into bits and making a layer of tiny green specks on the ground which were the bits that had fallen off the branches. And that strong smell of the sea. And I put my hand over my eyes. And I wondered why they called stenches stenches and smells smells and why they couldn't call the stenches smells and the smells stenches and I smelled Antoni's smell when he was awake and his smell when he was sleeping.

And I told Quimet that maybe instead of working from the outside in the termites worked from the inside out and stuck their heads out those little round holes and thought of all the damage they'd done. And how the children smelled like milk and saliva when they were little: fresh milk and milk that had gone sour. And Senyora Enriqueta always told me we had many interwoven lives and sometimes but not always a death or marriage separated them. And life itself, free from the threads of those little lives that tied it down, could keep on living by itself the way it would have had to do if all those bad little lives hadn't bothered it. And she said those little interwoven lives fight and torture us and we don't know what's going on just like we don't know how hard our hearts work or how our guts suffer. . . . And the smell of the sheets full of my body and Antoni's body, the smell of tired sheets soaking up someone's smells, the smell of their hair on the pillow, the smell of the little bits of dirt from their feet at the foot of the bed, the smell of the clothes they've worn and left overnight on a chair . . . And the smell of grain and potatoes and a big bottle of hydrochloric acid.

The knife had a wooden handle with three tacks through it with their heads flattened into the wood so the blade wouldn't come unstuck. I had my shoes in my hand and when I reached the courtyard I shut the balcony door and something kept pulling me along but it didn't come from inside or outside, and I leaned against a pillar so I could put my shoes on without falling. . . . I thought I heard the first cart far away, still half lost out there in the middle of the night that was ending. . . . Some leaves rustled on the peach tree, bathed in light from the streetlamp, and some bird's wings flew away. A branch swayed. The sky was dark blue and you could see the two buildings on the other side of the street with their porches facing each other and outlined against that high blue. I felt like I'd already done what I was doing sometime before but I didn't know when or where, like everything was growing out of roots in some time without memory. . . . I touched my face and it was still mine with my skin and my nose and my cheekbone, but even though it was me everything seemed covered with fog but not dead, as if clouds and clouds of dust had settled on it. . . . Before I reached the market and after the shop with the dolls I turned left toward the Carrer Gran.

And when I got to the Carrer Gran I crossed the sidewalk from one stone to another till I reached that long stone on the curb, and I stood there like a wooden statue with all kinds of things pulsing up from my heart to my head. A streetcar went by. It must have been the first one to leave the yards, a streetcar like all the others, old and faded—and maybe that same streetcar had seen me and Quimet behind me the night we came dashing out of the Plaça del Diamant like a couple of crazy rats. And something kept sticking in my throat like a chick-pea that had gone down the wrong way. I felt dizzy and closed my eyes and the draft from the streetcar helped me keep moving like my life was moving ahead of me. And when I took that first step I could still see the streetcar that had gone by, shooting off red and blue sparks between its wheels and the tracks. I felt like a tightrope walker, not daring to look down and thinking every second I was going to fall, and I got to the other side gripping the knife and without seeing the blue lights. . . .

And when I reached the other side I turned around and looked back with my eyes and my entire soul and I could hardly believe it. I'd crossed the street. And I started walking for my old life till I reached my old building and stood under the bay window. . . . The door was locked. I looked up and saw Quimet in the middle of a field by the sea when I was pregnant with Toni and he gave me a blue flower and then laughed at me. I wanted to go upstairs to my apartment, to my roof, to the scales, touching them as I went by. . . . I'd gone in that door many years ago married to Quimet and I'd come out with the children behind me to marry Antoni. The street was ugly and the building was ugly and the pavement was only good for carts and horses. The streetlight was far away and the doorway was dark. I looked for the hole Quimet had made and I found it right away: plugged with cork right above the lock. And I started digging out bits of cork with the tip of my knife. And the bits of cork flew out. And I got all the cork out and then I realized I couldn't get in. My fingers wouldn't reach the cord to get it out so I could pull it and open the door. I should have brought a wire to make a hook. And I was going to start pounding on the door but then I thought it might make too much noise so I hit the wall and it hurt a lot. And I turned around and rested and I still felt like I had to do something. So I turned back to the door and took my knife and carved "Colometa" on it in big, deep letters.

And without thinking I started walking again and the walls carried me along more than my own footsteps and I turned into the Plaça del Diamant: an empty box made of old buildings with the sky for a top. And I saw some little shadows fly across the top and all the buildings started rippling like they were in a pool and someone was slowly stirring it and the walls on the buildings stretched upward and leaned towards each other and the hole at the top got smaller and started turning into a funnel and I felt something in my hand and it was Mateu's hand and a satin-tie dove landed on his shoulder and I'd never seen one before but its feathers shimmered like a rainbow and I heard a storm coming up like a whirlwind inside the funnel which was almost closed now and I covered my face with my arms to protect myself from I don't know what and I let out a hellish scream. A scream I must have been carrying around inside me for many years, so thick it was hard for it to get through my throat, and with that scream a little bit of nothing trickled out of my mouth, like a cockroach made of spit . . . and that bit of nothing that had lived so long trapped inside me was my youth and it flew off with a scream of I don't know what . . . letting go?

Someone touched my arm and I turned around calmly. It was an old man. He asked me if I was sick and I heard some balcony doors open. "Don't you feel well?" And an old couple came up and stood in front of me and there was a white shadow on the balcony. "It's all over now," I said. And more people came. They came slowly like the daylight. And I said I was okay, it was all over. Just nerves, nothing, no danger. . . . And I started walking back the way I'd come. I turned around to look at the old man and woman. They'd stayed where they were, and in the pale light that was coming up now I felt like I was imagining them. . . . Thanks. Thanks. Thanks. Antoni had spent years thanking me and I'd never thanked him for anything. Thanks . . .

When I reached the curb on the Carrer Gran I looked both ways to make sure no streetcars were coming and then ran across and when I got to the other side I turned around again to look and see if that bit of nothing that had driven me crazy for so many years was following me. But I was alone. You could see the colors on the buildings and things. Carts and trucks were going up and down the streets that led to the market square and the men from the slaughterhouse were going into the market with bloodstained coats and calves cut in half slung across their shoulders. The florists were putting bunches of flowers in metal vases. The chrysanthemums gave off a bitter smell. The wasps' nest was coming to life.

And I turned into my street, the one that early morning cart always went down. And as I passed the shop entrances I looked in one where years ago a man had sold peaches and pears and soft plums and weighed them on old-fashioned scales with gold and iron weights. On scales he held up by sticking his finger through a hook at the top. And there were straw and wood chips and dirty crumpled pieces of tissue paper on the ground. No thanks. And the last birds shrieked in the sky above as they flew off shimmering into the shimmering blue. I stopped in front of the gate. The back porches were there, one on top of the other like niches in some strange cemetery with those green blinds you pull up with a cord, some pulled up and others left down. There were clothes hung out to dry and a spot of color here and there from a geranium in a pot.

I entered the courtyard just as a pathetic little ray of sunlight speckled the leaves on the peach tree. And I saw Antoni waiting for me at the balcony doors with his nose pressed against the glass. And I deliberately walked slowly, first one foot and then the other, and made my way across the courtyard. . . . My feet carried me along and they were feet that had done a lot of walking and maybe when I was dead Rita would stick them together with a safety pin so they wouldn't come apart. And Antoni opened the balcony doors and his voice was trembling as he asked me, "What happened?" and he said he'd woken up with a start as if someone had warned him that something terrible was going to happen and I wasn't there beside him and he couldn't find me anywhere. And I said, "Your feet are going to get cold . . ." and how I'd woken up when it was still dark out and hadn't been able to get back to sleep and I needed some fresh air because something was choking me. . . . He went back to bed without saying a word. "We can still get some sleep," I told him, and I looked at him from the back with the hairs on his neck a little too long and his sad, white ears that always got even whiter when he was cold. . . .

I put the knife down on the console and started getting undressed. First I closed the shutters and a little crack of daylight came through, and I went over to the bed and sat down and took off my shoes. The mattress creaked a little because it was old and two springs needed fixing. I pulled off my stockings like I was pulling off a very long skin and put my footwarmers on and then I realized I was frozen. I put on my nightgown, faded from so many washings. I buttoned it all the way up to the neck, straightened it, and buttoned the cuffs. I got into bed and tucked myself in, making sure the nightgown came down to my feet. And I said, "It's nice out."

The bed was warm as a greenfinch's belly but Antoni was shivering. I could hear his teeth chattering. He had his back to me and I slipped my arm under his arm and hugged his chest. I was still cold. I wrapped my legs around his legs and my feet around his feet and moved my hand lower and undid the button on his waist so he could breathe easier. I put my cheek against his back, against those little round bones, and I felt like I could hear everything alive inside him, which was all him too: first his heart and his lungs and his liver all soaked in juice and blood. And I started rubbing his belly slowly because he was my little cripple, and with my head against his back I thought how I didn't want him to die and I wanted to tell him everything I thought because I thought more than I said and I thought things you can't tell anyone and I didn't say anything and gradually my feet warmed up and we fell asleep like that and before I fell asleep as I was rubbing his belly my finger bumped into his belly button and I stuck it inside to stop it up so he wouldn't empty out. . . . "We're all like pears when we're born. . . ." So he wouldn't slip off like a stocking. So no evil witch would suck him out through his belly button and leave me without Antoni. . . .

And that's how we fell asleep: slowly, like two heavenly angels, and he slept till eight in the morning and I slept through to noon. . . . And I woke up after sleeping like a rock and my mouth had a dry, bitter taste in it and it was different from other nights because the morning was noon and I got up and started getting dressed as usual without knowing what I was doing because my soul was still in the shell of my dreams. And I stood there with my hands on the sides of my head and I knew I'd done something different but I had trouble remembering what I'd done and whether I'd done what I'd done—and I didn't even know if I'd done it—half awake or fast asleep till I washed my face and the water woke me up and put the color back in my cheeks and the light in my eyes. . . .

It was too late to have breakfast. I just took a sip of water to get the burning taste out of my mouth. . . . The water was cold and I remembered how the morning before when it was time for the wedding it had rained hard and I thought maybe that afternoon when I went to the park like usual there'd still be a puddle in one of the paths . . . and in every puddle, no matter how small, the sky . . . a sky shattered from time to time by a bird . . . a bird who was thirsty and without realizing it shattered the sky in the water with his beak . . . or a bunch of chattering birds who'd fly down from the leaves like lightning bolts and dive into the puddle and swim around with their feathers all ruffled and mix up the sky with mud and beaks and wings. Happy . . .

Geneva, February–September, 1960